SUMMER HEAT

JULY by Pamela Burford

Molly Lamb was Quinn Marshall's upstairs neighbor from hell. First of all, she stayed up half the night making an infernal racket. Secondly, she was the runaway bride of his former boss. And thirdly, this uninhibited nature girl showered naked outside. It was more than a man could take! But Molly's idea of being neighborly left Quinn no choice but to get up close and *very* personal.

AUGUST by Patricia Ryan

When Sally Curran first laid eyes on Tom O'Hearn she saw a gorgeous hunk that she wouldn't touch with a ten-foot pole. He was definitely not serious-relationship material, this handyman whose office was a truck. But…they *were* sharing a beach house for a month…and the chemistry between them *was* volcanic. A little summer fling wouldn't hurt. She didn't have to fall in love or anything…did she?

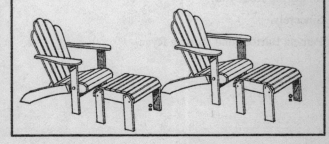

Dear Reader,

As identical twins, we've always been close, and now that we're both romance authors, we share a very special bond. Though we have our own independent writing careers, working together on special projects like *Summer Heat* is especially rewarding. Who better to collaborate with than your twin sister?

The setting for these two stories is one we're both intimately familiar with. Our families shared this Cape Cod beach house twice, and we have wonderful memories of our time on the bay. No, the actual house is not as decrepit as the one described in these pages—we exercised our creative license!

These novellas offer the kind of light, lively summer stories we like to read at the beach or on the back porch with a tall glass of iced tea after a long day at work. We hope you have as much fun reading them as we did writing them!

We've joined the computer age and now have home pages on the web. You can get to them by visiting Harlequin's web site (http://www.romance.net) and clicking on our names in the author list. We look forward to hearing from you!

Sincerely,

Pamela Burford and Patricia Ryan

SUMMER HEAT
Pamela Burford & Patricia Ryan

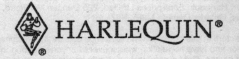

HARLEQUIN®

TORONTO • NEW YORK • LONDON
AMSTERDAM • PARIS • SYDNEY • HAMBURG
STOCKHOLM • ATHENS • TOKYO • MILAN • MADRID
PRAGUE • WARSAW • BUDAPEST • AUCKLAND

To our mother, Sue Burford

ISBN 0-373-25796-1

SUMMER HEAT

JULY
Copyright © 1998 by Pamela Loeser.

AUGUST
Copyright © 1998 by Patricia Burford Ryan.

July

by
Pamela Burford

1

QUINN MARSHALL had never seen a naked woman outdoors before. That realization only came to him later. For now, his brain was incapable of forging a thought, having gone on strike the instant he'd rounded the back of Phil's beach house and spotted the stranger rinsing off under the outdoor shower, situated at the far end of the wooden, wraparound deck.

She was unaware of his presence—correction, *blissfully* unaware. Eyes squeezed shut against the hammering spray, she was dancing to her own off-key if spirited rendition of Gloria Gaynor's "I Will Survive."

And that was something else, Quinn would later reflect. He'd never before seen a naked woman dance, much less with this degree of unselfconscious enthusiasm. And no, Phil's bachelor party didn't count.

What she lacked in vocal skills, she more than made up for in heart and a healthy sense of rhythm. She was a disco dynamo, from the undulating hips to the shimmying shoulders and breasts, tipped by nipples so tightly puckered they looked like pink berries.

Which prompted his first coherent thought, that the water had to be cold. Either that or this lady was *really* into disco. He was just close enough to see gooseflesh everywhere he looked. And he looked everywhere.

Quinn's innate sense of propriety finally kicked in, ending his brief foray into voyeurism. He commenced an awkward backward shuffle, powerless to drag his gaze from the spectacle.

The air left his lungs in an astonished bark as he landed hard on his butt on the sandy lawn. Beach paraphernalia clattered out of the plastic tote basket he'd tripped over. "I Will Survive" ended on a high-pitched yelp. The shower stopped. Cursing under his breath, Quinn struggled to pry his foot out of the basket handle.

"You surprised me!" the woman said with a breathless chuckle. She lifted a vividly colored beach towel from the deck and started blotting her face. "You must be my downstairs neighbor."

"Uh…yeah." Quinn managed to wrench the basket off his foot, but his deck shoe went with it. He shoved the shoe back on his bare foot while racking his brain for words appropriate to this situation. *Please forgive me for inadvertently witnessing your display of public nudity and enjoying it.*

"I just got here this morning," she said, squeezing water from her waist-length brown hair. "I leased the upstairs for the month of July."

Her attitude couldn't have been more blasé, while Quinn felt a scalding flush crawl up his throat. He staggered to his feet and brushed sand off his khaki shorts.

She started toward him, briskly toweling her chest and arms. "I'm Molly. How long are you staying?"

She stuck out her hand, and automatically he shook it. It was icy from the cold shower.

I'm shaking a naked lady's hand. There's a naked lady standing here and I'm shaking her hand.

He cleared his throat. "Quinn Marshall. Nice to meet you."

"That is such a great name! Welcome, Quinn."

Molly's smiling eyes were sapphire **blue**, shading to violet near the center with a dark ring around the iris. There was a little mole under the outside corner of her left eye. She squinted just a bit against the moisture that spiked her lashes, giving her a slumberous, just-been-loved look.

None of which would have registered, he knew, if he hadn't been staring fixedly into her eyes in a heroic effort to keep from staring anywhere else.

She bent down to dry her legs, looking up with an expectant expression that reminded Quinn she'd asked him something.

He said, "Uh...I have the place all month. Yeah. Till August first. Well. Not the whole place. Just the downstairs. Not the upstairs. I mean, well, you know, you have the upstairs, right?" *Shut up*, he commanded himself. *Shut! Up!*

"Oh, listen, does this bother you?" Molly straightened, with an open-armed gesture meant to draw his attention to those parts of her he was studiously trying to ignore. A few lingering droplets of water quivered between her breasts and in the triangle of dark hair at the juncture of her thighs.

"No!" He shooed away the ludicrous idea and struck what he hoped was an indolent pose.

"I sometimes forget that most people are a little, you know, uptight about their bodies." As she spoke, she slid the big, colorful towel behind her back, wrapped both sides over her front and tied the top corners behind her neck. It looked like some sort of psychedelic toga.

Quinn had known there would be another tenant, in the second floor of the duplex house, but where had Phil dug up this flaky exhibitionist? Was this little town in Cape Cod some kind of clothing-optional vacation spot and no one had seen fit to inform him?

No distractions, his friends had said. They'd assured him this vacation would be just what he needed, a few weeks of solitary R and R to evaluate his options, fine-tune his resumé and chart his next career move—hopefully with better results than last time.

Quinn had had to take their word for it. What did he know about vacations? He could count on one hand the number of times he'd taken so much as a weekend off during the past eight years he'd spent clawing his way up the corporate ladder in the advertising business.

Two weeks ago he'd taken an unexpected tumble off that ladder when he'd lost his job as executive account manager at Phil Owen and Associates. The fact that Phil had been forced to let him go due to a business merger didn't make unemployment any easier to stomach. Quinn had been with the agency only four months, but nobody could say he hadn't been doing a damn fine job.

Knowing better than to burn his bridges, he remained on amicable terms with his ex-boss. Even so, when Phil had offered him free use of the first floor of his Cape Cod beach house for a month—probably out of feelings of guilt—Quinn's first instinct had been to refuse.

His buddies had had other ideas. They'd urged him to take a little time off before leaping back into the job market. Chill-out time, they'd called it. The critical component? No distractions. They'd been quite firm on that point.

He'd only known Molly a minute or two, but he doubted he'd ever been more distracted.

She walked past him around the house, which was sided in weathered gray cedar shakes that had seen better days. "I'll help you bring your stuff into the house."

"Oh, thanks, but that's not—"

"Wow! Nice car!"

He rounded the corner to find her running her hand over the gleaming fender of his new Mercedes, the only car occupying the crushed-shell parking area. He wondered where hers was.

"It is the *exact* color of butter!" She leaned over the hood, stroking his vehicle as if it were a lover. "Pale and creamy, the perfect yellow, you know? Classy."

As she straightened, her long wet hair trailed over the freshly waxed surface. Judging from his physical reaction, it might as well have been trailing over his bare thighs.

He quickly circled the car, unlocked the trunk and hauled out his burgundy leather garment bag and matching suitcase. She joined him and hefted the plastic milk crate crammed with coffee, sugar and other staples he'd brought from his Manhattan apartment.

"No, I mean it," he said. "I can do this."

"You're really tense, Quinn," she observed pleasantly as she led the way to the front door. "Stiff, you know?"

He knew. But thanks to loose shorts and an untucked polo shirt, maybe *she* didn't have to. He followed her with the luggage. The toga-towel thing covered her modestly to her knees, but it hugged her form in a way he could only describe as, well, distracting.

Tucking the milk crate under one arm, Molly opened the front door, which was desperately in need of a new coat of paint, and stood aside to let him enter the vestibule. To the left was a locked door that obviously led to his portion of the house. Directly ahead was a scarred wooden staircase to the upper floor, which Molly had rented. The door at the top had a lock, but at the moment it stood wide open. Quinn set down the luggage, dug in his pocket for the keys Phil had given him and unlocked the inner door.

Phil had described the place as a bare-bones beach house, and he hadn't lied. The living room and dining area sported an eclectic assortment of functional, if shabby, furniture. The floor was brown vinyl tiles, warped and peeling in the high-traffic areas. Tacky seaside prints adorned the fake-wood paneling. The inside of the place was as dilapidated as the outside, but at least it was reasonably clean, and it was all his, free of charge, for the month of July.

Yep. Thirty-one days to just relax, kick back and try to decide what he really wanted out of life. An entire month. No work. No urban hustle and bustle. No work. No know-it-all pals spouting unsolicited advice. No work.

If he left now, he could make it back to the city before dinner.

"It's not that bad," Molly said, clearly misinterpreting his expression. She shrugged and shifted the crate to the other arm. "Nothing fancy, but at least you don't have to worry about trashing the place, right?"

There was that luminous smile again, as if she didn't have a care in the world. Perhaps she didn't. Perhaps Mellow Molly was as shallow and uncomplicated as first appearances suggested.

"Hey, Quinn, check it out! You've got tunes!" She crossed to the ponderous sideboard and set the crate next to a little record player, one of those cheap old portable models built into a pressboard carrying box. Next to it sat a stack of ancient LPs in cardboard sleeves held together with brittle yellowed tape.

Quinn said, "We've entered a time warp."

"Fifties and sixties, it looks like," she said, flipping through the albums. "Too early for disco, but it's still great stuff. The Supremes, Chuck Berry, Buddy Holly and the Crickets. Looks like somebody bought a CD player on vacation and abandoned their old friends. How sad. The Jackson Five, James Brown, the Ronettes—'Be My Baby,' I *love* that song. Jerry Lee Lewis, the Shirelles."

She gazed fondly at an album cover. "Bill Haley and the Comets. I mean, how can you not love a group with a name like that? The Isley Brothers, the Marvelettes. Oh wow! Little Richard!"

Molly tipped out the album, set it on the turntable and turned on the machine. She positioned the needle on a groove in the vinyl. Static spewed from the tinny, built-in speaker as both Little Richard and

Molly *awahbahbaloomah*ed into the opening of "Tutti Frutti."

As she sang, she performed the twist, gyrating low enough to make the towel gape alarmingly as it rode up her thighs. *American Bandstand* was never like this. When Little Richard got to the part about the girl named Daisy who almost drove him crazy, Molly let him continue solo.

"Whoo!" She fanned herself with her hand. "You are, like, *so lucky*, Quinn!" She hefted the crate once more and carried it through an archway into what he could only assume was the kitchen. "I don't have any music upstairs," she called out. "Just my trumpet."

Quinn heard cupboards and drawers open and close, the rattle of flatwear and dishes. He headed for the vestibule to get his luggage.

Just her trumpet. *Yes*, Quinn thought, *I am, like, so lucky*.

"You've got more cooking stuff than I do!" she hollered. "And it's newer, too. Guess we'll be eating down here a lot."

He froze in the process of lifting his bags. *We?* He entered the living room just as Molly headed down the hallway toward the bedrooms.

"You're here alone?" she asked.

"Uh, Molly—"

"Me, too. Each level has three bedrooms. You'll want the one at the end of the hall. It's the biggest and has its own bathroom. Well, half bath. You'll have to shower in the hall john." She let herself into the master bedroom and hurled herself onto the bare double bed. "This is where I'll be staying."

He took a moment to find his voice. "Excuse me?"

Molly pointed to the ceiling. "Upstairs. I took the same room. You'll be sleeping right under me!" She looked at him quickly. "Oh, listen, I hope that didn't sound, you know, suggestive or anything."

"No!" he said, trying to sound convincing.

She smiled in relief. "Good. Sometimes I say something and then I think, gosh, could *that* ever be taken the wrong way!" She bounced vigorously on the bed a few times. "You may have a melon baller, Quinn, but I've got better support. My springs squeak like crazy, though."

She jumped off the bed and headed into the bathroom. With the morbid fascination of a storm watcher tracking a lethal tornado, Quinn moved to the doorway and watched her inspect the half bath, about the size of an airplane lavatory. It featured rust-stained white porcelain and broken hinges on the under-the-sink cabinet.

"Don't tell me," he said. "Upstairs you have a marble vanity, a Jacuzzi and a gold-plated bidet."

She whirled on him with a delighted grin. "You have a sense of humor!"

Quinn took a deep breath. "Molly, uh, when you said you guessed we'd be eating down here...well, what exactly did you—"

"I meant since it's just the two of us, you know?" Without warning, she started to squeeze past him through the narrow bathroom doorway. He held his breath and smiled awkwardly and tried to make himself very flat. Her warmth and the scent of her wrapped around him, a blend of coconut oil, the briny sea and her own elusive feminine essence.

Pressed belly-to-belly with him, she paused and

said, "I don't know about you, but I hate eating alone."

"I myself don't mind it," he croaked.

She shrugged, with an agreeable smile, and scooted past him. "That's cool. Let me know if you change your mind."

He followed her down the hall, unaccountably disappointed that she'd given up so easily.

Which was asinine in the extreme. Not that he was averse to a diverting summer romp, but in this case diverting could turn into disastrous. He and Molly had to share this house for a whole month. Just long enough for a little harmless fun to balloon into some kind of tedious overblown entanglement, complete with tears, tantrums and recriminations. *Fatal Attraction*, Cape Cod style.

While Little Richard screeched something unintelligible from the living room, Quinn silently chanted his mantra du jour. *No distractions, no distractions.*

At the doorway Molly turned. "You will not want to miss the sunset, Quinn. Everyone congregates on the beach to watch the sun sink into the bay. It's like that whole Key West thing, but without the hype, you know?"

"Wait. I thought you said you just got here this morning."

"I did."

"So how do you know about the sunset thing?"

"Oh, Phil and I used to stay here whenever we could get away, and we never missed a sunset. This place might not be the height of luxury or anything, but I'm telling you, the location can't be beat. It's the last house before the beach, so it's, like, a thirty-second walk to the water. What?" She eyed Quinn curiously as comprehension whacked him on the noggin.

He said, "You're Molly!"

"Didn't I say that?"

"*Phil's* Molly."

"Well, not anymore. But yeah, I'm Molly Lamb. So how do you know Phil? I figured you found this place through the local realtor he uses."

"I work for him. Worked," he corrected. "Until two weeks ago."

"You quit?"

"Uh, no."

A surprised smile lit her face. "Then we have something in common. He fired me, too!"

"Yeah, I know that."

"Oh, that's right, I guess everyone does, huh?"

She could have been talking about the latest summer movie. Did *anything* get to this woman?

She laid a hand on his arm. "It was *so* nice meeting you, Quinn. Listen, I just know you're going to have a fabulous vacation here. It's like magic, this house! And hey, I'm not kidding about that sunset. Will I see you there?"

He nodded woodenly.

"All right!" A playful slap on his shoulder and she was gone, springing up the stairs.

Quinn locked his door, trudged into the living room and flopped onto the rump-sprung sofa. Little Richard began hollering his way through "Good Golly Miss Molly."

It was a big house, but it wasn't that big. How was Quinn supposed to avoid Phil Owen's runaway bride for a whole damn month?

2

THERE WAS THAT odd pounding again. Molly paused to listen, the silver-plated trumpet poised at her lips. The noise from downstairs stopped. She shrugged and resumed her playing, improvising around her favorite New Orleans jazz riffs.

There it was again! What was Quinn doing down there, heavy construction? The living room floor quaked under her feet.

Molly moved to the top of the stairs and called down, "Quinn!" Belatedly remembering he'd locked his door, she smiled. You could take the boy out of the city…

Horn in hand, she descended the stairs and knocked on his door. She heard movement, sensed him hesitating on the other side. Finally the lock turned and the door eased open a scant few inches. A heavenly aroma drifted out, something spicy with a base of sautéed onions and garlic.

She looked up into those gray-green, heavy-lidded eyes, framed by lush black lashes—and felt the same giddy jolt that had struck her earlier that day when they'd first met. These were the voluptuous eyes of a practiced gigolo, or an imperious sheik with carnal intent and his choice of slave girls. Not some uptight ad exec on holiday.

She chalked it up to one of Mother Nature's little practical jokes.

"Quinn, what're you doing to the ceiling? Exterminating termites with a baseball bat?" Through the narrow opening she saw he held something in his hand. A broom. He *was* pounding on the ceiling! "Oh, wait. Is that about this?" She held up the trumpet.

The door opened fractionally wider and she saw he was barefoot and bare chested, wearing only thin gray sweatpants. His expression was tightly shuttered, revealing the barest whiff of annoyance. He said, "It's after midnight."

She leaned on the door frame. "Yeah, but I heard you moving around down here, so I knew you hadn't gone to bed. What, was my playing bothering you?"

"It's a little late to be blasting away on a trumpet, don't you think?"

"No. Since you ask." She grinned. "That pounding on the ceiling—that's such a *city* thing! Why didn't you just come up and ask me to stop? If it was bothering you."

"I didn't say it was...." He looked away. Pushed his fingers through his short black hair. "You play quite well, actually."

"Thanks. But if you want me to stop..."

"No. This is stupid." He glanced at the broom in his hand, clearly chagrined. "I guess it was just..."

"Force of habit?" She smiled.

His mouth quirked. "I guess so."

"What're you cooking? It smells outrageous!" She stuck her head in the door, pushing it wider.

"*Chili con queso.* Hot cheese dip."

"No kidding!" She squeezed past him and headed into the kitchen, where the concoction—orange melted cheese with specks of red tomato, green jalapeño and golden onions—bubbled in a cast-iron frying pan. "A sense of humor *and* he cooks! Marry me, Quinn."

He said, "I guess there's enough for two. Can I, uh, get you something to drink?"

"Oh, I'm terrible, aren't I, barging in here and making myself at home. Beer, if you have it." She opened the refrigerator and perused the contents. "Quinn, I thought you went shopping today." He'd gone for a drive and returned with sacks from the supermarket.

"I have beer." He crossed the room, opened a couple of high cupboards and pulled down a bag of tortilla chips and a heavy stoneware bowl. Molly enjoyed watching him move, with an easy masculine grace that she doubted he was aware of.

She'd known Quinn had a nice body even before seeing him half-naked like this. Despite that loose polo shirt he'd worn earlier, her eagle eye had detected firm pecs, a flat belly and world-class shoulders that she now struggled not to stare at too blatantly. Molly liked shoulders.

"But that's about all you have," she said. "Beer. Soda. Bottled water. A quart of milk. What, are you on a liquids-only diet?"

"Look in the freezer." As he carried the food into the living room, she just made out his muttered "since you're taking inventory."

"TV dinners? Quinn, you've got a *barbecue grill* out there on the deck! Didn't you see it?"

"There's also a microwave. It's easier. You gonna come eat this or not?"

"It's not about easy. It's about *summer*. It's about the *Cape*. Gosh, it's not like you don't know how to cook!"

She opened her beer and joined him in the living room, where she carefully placed her trumpet on the sideboard before flopping onto the end of the sofa and stretching her legs out on the cushions.

She, too, was barefoot, dressed in a white, spaghetti-strap top with a huge sunflower design on the front, and denim cutoffs short enough for the bottoms of the pockets to peek out under the frayed hem. Quinn sat on one of the well-worn easy chairs, his slightly stiff posture at odds with his state of dishabille.

Leaning toward the wooden coffee table, she reached for a chip and scooped up a gob of dip.

"Careful," he said. "That's hot."

She blew on it and popped it in—and applied a therapeutic mouthful of cold beer as the melted cheese scalded the roof of her mouth. When she could speak again, she said, "I'm impatient. Is that a sign of immaturity, do you think? Being unable to delay gratification?"

Quinn appeared to give that some thought as he loosened the cap on his bottle of spring water. "I don't know you well enough to say. Do *you* think it's a sign of immaturity?"

Gosh, she'd been kidding—just trying to make conversation. Sense of humor or no, this was one serious guy!

He continued, "As far as immaturity goes, there

are more clear-cut indicators. Like irresponsibility. Failure to live up to one's commitments."

He left that hanging there, those gigolo eyes peering at her from under thick dark brows as he reached for a chip. Then she got it.

Phil. The wedding.

"I know what you must've heard," she said. "What Phil must be saying about me."

"He didn't have to say anything. I was there."

"Where? At the church, you mean?"

He nodded.

"That looked bad, I know," she said.

"Leaving your groom standing at the altar? What do you think?"

"He wasn't actually standing at the altar!"

"Close enough. The wedding march was playing, Molly. You never showed."

"I showed. Is that what he told everyone? That I never even made it to the church?" Molly sat up crossed-legged, all ears, fascinated to learn what Phil was saying about her.

Quinn paused in the act of dipping a chip, as if her eager attentiveness confounded him. "Well, that was the impression. Phil didn't make the announcement himself, of course. His brother Ron—he was the best man—"

"Nice guy, Ron," she said. "Heck of a poker player. Tried to teach me to bluff, but I'm not very good at it."

"Ron stopped the organ music and told all the guests that the wedding was canceled. That the bride had backed out."

Molly lifted her beer. "Well, that's true. I did."

He stared at her. "How can you be so blasé about it?"

"It was four months ago, Quinn. I'm over it."

"*You're* over it!" He sat forward, his face darkening. "What about Phil? The grief you caused him. The humiliation."

"Do you want to hear my side?"

He sat back. "No."

"I didn't think so," she said pleasantly. "People are comfortable with what they know, you know? Or what they think they know. Why did Phil fire you?"

The abrupt question rendered him momentarily speechless. Gosh, she hadn't meant to embarrass him. Her and her big mouth!

"I mean, you're obviously still on good terms with him," she said. "That's so important, not to hold a grudge. Too many people, they can't get past their ego, you know? Especially guys. This chili is *fabulous*. You've gotta teach me how to make it."

"It was purely a business decision," Quinn said tightly. "It's not like I was let go for cause or anything. You must know about the merger with Glacken and Ross. Massive reorganization. Unfortunately, I was one of the casualties. Phil felt rotten about it, but it's not like he had a choice."

"How long did you work there?"

"Four months."

"You must've joined just after I left. I took off the last couple of weeks before the wedding to get ready, do all the last-minute preparations. It was going to be like this huge fairy-tale production. You should've seen my gown—I felt like Cinderella at the ball."

Until she dragged her train through dirt and gravel, crammed the voluminous ivory silk into the driver's seat of her sister Toni's battered, two-tone Honda hatchback and burned rubber out of the church parking lot. Tears had smeared her vision until she'd finally pulled off the highway and brought up her breakfast in a stand of winter brown forsythia.

Quinn was looking at her with a strange intensity that made Molly wonder if he sensed the direction of her thoughts. She willed the memory back into its dark little cave. Nothing good came of dwelling on the hurt.

"So," she said. "You must still be tight with Phil to rent part of his beach house for the month."

Quinn opened his mouth as if to amend her statement, and hesitated. "Like you said, no point in holding a grudge. You, on the other hand—I must admit, I'm surprised you'd want to stay here, all things considered. And, frankly, just as surprised Phil agreed to it."

"Well, he knows how much I love this house, and the Cape. We spent so much time here, so many long weekends. I just knew this was where I had to come to collect my thoughts, to find myself, you know? It's like this house was calling to me. It's worth every penny."

Quinn looked as if he wanted to ask her something but knew he shouldn't. He did it anyway. "How much is he charging you?"

"Nine hundred fifty bucks."

His eyebrows rose. "Sweet deal. He must still have a soft spot for you somewhere, Molly. This place is pretty rundown, but he could get a lot more than nine fifty a month."

"Oh, that's per week." The chili was congealing fast. She troweled a glob onto a chip.

"Wait a minute. Phil's charging you nine-fifty a *week*? That's—that's thirty-eight hundred for the month!"

"Well, more, really. The month is four and a half weeks. But it's still a bargain. He usually gets well over a thousand a week."

"That's what he told you?"

"Uh-huh. Why? What's he charging you?"

Quinn lifted his bottle of spring water. Took a long swallow. Set it back down. "No offense, but I don't like discussing my finances."

"Just other people's." At his sharp look she laughed and hurled a throw pillow at him. "Just kidding! You gotta loosen up, Quinn. You're on vacation!"

He said, "You were a copy editor for Phil's firm, right?"

She grunted "Mm-hmm" around a mouthful of food.

"I take it you haven't found another position?"

"Job market's tough. I figure if nothing full-time opens up when I get back, I can always do freelance." She ran a chip along the inside of the bowl, scraping off the last of the chili.

"But don't you have expenses, an apartment to pay for?"

"You're so sweet to be concerned about me! I don't have anything left in the bank, but thank heaven for plastic. Without that cash advance, I wouldn't be here this summer."

"You financed this vacation with a *credit card?*"

"So?" She drained the last of her beer.

"So with—what? Something like twenty-one percent interest added to your costs—"

"You're very analytical, you know that? Sometimes you have to just put aside all the day-to-day stuff that grinds you down and open yourself up to, well, *this*." She spread her arms wide, indicating the beach, the bay, the whole darn gorgeous, curvaceous Cape, from Falmouth to Provincetown.

"Even when you'll be paying off *this* for months or years to come, with no money in the bank and no job prospects?"

"I didn't mean to give you something else to worry about." She waved off his concerns. "I'll be fine. Things have a way of working out."

"What do you mean, something *else* to worry about? I'm not worried about anything." Quinn settled deeper into his chair, crossed his ankle over his knee and sighed gustily. He looked about as relaxed as a novice snake handler.

"Well, you're out of work, too, right?" she asked.

"Not for long. If I'd stayed home, I'd have the whole job thing wrapped up this week. This wasn't my idea, coming up here to 'chill out' and all that." His fingers drummed on his leg.

"Well, whoever's idea it was, it was a good one. Just you wait and see. The thing is, you have to embrace it, Quinn. Which it doesn't look like you're doing. I mean, I thought you were going to watch the sunset with everyone this evening."

"I did!"

"For, like, a whole two seconds."

Quinn shrugged. "It's a sunset. How long can you stand there and watch a thing like that?"

She wagged her finger, smiling. "You'll get it. One

of these days before you go home it'll sneak up on you and you'll just get it." She stood up. "Meanwhile, it's late and you're out of chili."

She planted her palms on the small of her back and arched her spine, stretching, groaning lustily as she felt her muscles unkink. Quinn's fingers stopped drumming. He became very still, though his expression never changed. As she watched him watching her, the tips of Molly's breasts buzzed, springing to attention under her thin little shirt. He noticed, and for a few breathless moments she felt like one of those slave girls presented for the sheik's inspection. *Turn around. Take this off. Dance for me.*

Gosh! Both her big mouth and her imagination were getting a healthy workout tonight!

"Thanks for the chili," she said, breaking the spell. "And the beer." She started collecting the remains of their repast.

He leaped out of his chair and grabbed the chip bowl out of her hands. "Leave this. I'll take care of it."

"Listen, maybe we could barbecue together tomorrow. I have dogs and chicken, potato salad, the works. Bring a couple of those—" she nodded toward the beer bottle "—and we're set."

His features settled into a polite mask. "Thanks for the offer, but I really do prefer to eat alone."

"Oh."

"I'm kind of, uh, looking forward to a few weeks of just being on my own."

"Oh. Right."

"No obligations. No...distractions."

Embarrassment prickled like a rash. Here she'd barged her way into this guy's personal space, eaten

his food, drunk his beer—criticized his whole outlook on life, for heaven's sake!—when all the poor
man wanted was to be left alone.

"No problem," she said, backing toward the door.
"Good night."

"Don't forget your trumpet." He handed it to her.

Molly slowly climbed the stairs, trudged into her
living room and flung herself on the sofa, hugging
her horn to her chest.

Thirty-one days. How was she supposed to avoid
her uptight housemate with the gigolo eyes and the
yummy shoulders for a whole damn month?

3

THE BAY WAS PLUMP and placid at high tide, infinitely easier to swim in than the Atlantic Ocean a short distance away right across the Cape. To Quinn's way of thinking, the only drawback to being on the bay side was the distinctive aroma at low tide, but after the first day or two, he no longer noticed it.

He'd been doing the crawl for about forty-five minutes and could feel it in his shoulders. If this were a pool, he'd be able to calculate distance. As it was, he could only guess, which was mildly irksome.

He changed direction and headed for shore. If his buddies could read his thoughts right now, they'd write him off as hopelessly rigid. Or analytical—wasn't that how Molly had put it? According to his laid-back housemate and his pals back home, he was supposed to be using this time to chill out, to find his inner beach bum or some such garbage.

Meanwhile he was itching to get back to the city and set the job-hunting wheels in motion. One thing he'd never been good at was wasting time.

Quinn waded onto the hot sand and headed for his towel, where he'd left his keys, sunglasses and plastic thongs. With the house so near the beach, there was no need to bring more. Molly was right. It was a phenomenal location.

Today only a few wisps of cloud scudded across

the azure sky, and the temperature was a comfortable mid-eighties. The strip of beach was narrow, backed by a clifflike dune, and he shared it with a couple of dozen other folks, mainly couples and families with young children.

He toweled off, slipped on his shades and made his way down the beach and up a gentle incline to the tiny parking lot where an ice cream truck now sat, surrounded by sand-encrusted kids waving dollar bills. He dropped the thongs and slipped them on, having learned his first day there what happened when the tender soles of one's feet met black asphalt that had been baking in the sun for a few hours.

Quinn crossed the little parking lot, nodding politely to the attendant sitting on a lawn chair, dutifully collecting five bucks from those not fortunate enough to live within walking distance. The house was right there on the left, and as always, Quinn scanned the grounds and the second-floor deck for signs of Molly.

As requested, she'd left him alone during the past week, though she was unfailingly cheerful and animated whenever their paths crossed. He hadn't enjoyed telling her to keep her distance. He knew he'd embarrassed her, but he also knew that a preemptive strike would be the least painful in the long run. For both of them.

Quinn was honest enough with himself to admit he was physically attracted to Molly Lamb—to a garrulous, relentlessly cheerful, unrepentant heartbreaker. This was, after all, the woman who'd bolted from her wedding four months earlier, making a fool out of one of the most powerful men in the advertising business.

Quinn had seen her on the beach every day, of course, dog-paddling around the bay, soaking up the rays in her sexy little swimsuits, chatting with the other beachgoers. While he himself hadn't exchanged two words with any of the people he saw there day after day, Molly had apparently become fast friends with each and every one of them. Her treks down the beach took forever. With all that glad-handing and baby kissing, one would think she were running for office!

She exchanged snacks with these people, kept an eye on their kids, and just that morning had even let some guy in a blond ponytail and a pair of tight red Speedos rub sunscreen on her!

Molly's innate friendliness and too-trusting nature were going to get her into trouble one of these days. Quinn found himself keeping an eye on her—for her own good. He'd tried to reconcile her ingenuous charm with her horrendous treatment of Phil Owen, and came up empty. Then again, you never knew what lay beneath the surface until you really got to know someone. Undoubtedly Phil was better off without her.

Charging her that exorbitant rent had to have been some kind of vindictive parting shot. True, the house was in a great location, but Phil had let it go to hell. The decks were rotting through in places, half the windows and sliding doors wouldn't budge, the plumbing was unreliable, the tile floors were buckling, the yard was overrun with poison ivy and some of the weathered cedar shakes needed to be replaced. And that yard-sale furniture! Phil could do a lot better, for a minimal investment. Quinn couldn't believe his paying tenants didn't complain.

He also couldn't believe anyone else paid what Phil was charging Molly. Given the house's present condition, Quinn doubted Phil could get more than seven hundred a week for each apartment at the peak of tourist season—eight hundred, tops.

This petty act of revenge lowered Quinn's opinion of his former boss. What kind of man would take such blatant advantage of his broke and ridiculously gullible ex-fiancée? Meanwhile he'd given Quinn—who could easily afford to buy the place outright—a free ride. Quinn had seen no point in letting Molly know that. He had no desire to get in the middle of something messy.

He cut across the street and front yard to the deck, where he flung his damp towel over a ratty lawn chair. The outdoor shower was located in back of the house at the far end of the wraparound deck, out of sight of the street. Quinn hadn't actually seen Molly use it since that first day, but he'd heard the water go on a couple of times when he was inside. He'd heard her belting out Donna Summers's "Last Dance" and the Bee Gees' "Staying Alive." For a guy with an admittedly feeble imagination, he'd had no trouble picturing her in painstaking detail, soaping up, rinsing off, dancing her little heart out.

He shuffled out of his thongs and bent to toss them onto the deck when a tinny *brrring-brrring* brought his head up. A bicycle bell. Molly was approaching the house on her rented bike. Two overstuffed plastic grocery sacks were crammed into the wire basket, with two more bags hanging off the handlebars. Another full sack dangled from her forearm. Her hair was secured in a long, thick braid that snaked out from under a bright blue bike helmet.

She spied him and raised her free arm to wave, just as she turned off the road onto the crushed-shell driveway. The bike wobbled violently and she grabbed the handlebar, too late. The tires skidded out from under her, sending her sprawling into the shell shards as bags split and groceries tumbled out around her.

Quinn had reached her before the wheels stopped spinning. "Don't move," he said. "Just stay there." She lay on her side, looking a little dazed. Thank goodness for the helmet. He tossed the bike aside and quickly checked for broken bones, grateful when he didn't find any. Still, her skimpy yellow tank top and cutoffs had provided scant protection, and she was badly scraped up.

"Wow," she breathed, reaching for the helmet straps, fumbling with the release catch, her fingers trembling. He brushed her hands away and gently removed the helmet. She struggled up onto her elbow, wincing, and he helped her to sit.

She looked at the broken eggs scattered about, the leaking milk container and crushed grapes. "My groceries."

"What were you thinking, carrying all that stuff on a bike?"

She gazed up at him with a look of such heartbreaking vulnerability that he felt instantly ashamed. "Never mind," he said, carefully brushing shell gravel from her abraded chin. "It's okay. Let's get you cleaned up. Think you can walk?"

"My groceries..." She stared at her scraped-up left knee, beginning to ooze blood in earnest, as were her chin, shoulder and elbow.

"I'll get your groceries, don't worry. First let's get you into the house."

He fished his keys from the pocket of his boxer-style swim trunks and unlocked the doors, then came back and scooped her into his arms. She opened her mouth as if to protest, but then relaxed against his bare chest.

Quinn felt something rip loose inside—an unaccustomed surge of protectiveness, as foreign and frightening as it was exhilarating. In his nearly thirty years on the planet, he'd never been responsible for anyone but himself.

He settled her in his arms and carried her into the house, past the living room with its scratchy sofa to the relative comfort of his bedroom. On the way, he lowered his head a fraction, teasing his lips with the gossamer-fine wisps of hair that had escaped her braid. He inhaled the fragrance of sun and shampoo and the clean humid warmth of her exertions. He'd thought her hair was brown, but now he saw it was shot through with golden strands.

Carefully he set her on the double bed, stacking the pillows behind her so she could recline comfortably. She looked at the crisply tucked bedcovers, the soft cotton blanket stretched tight and smooth beneath her. "You make your bed?"

"So?"

"So who's going to see it?"

"Today? You."

That earned a weak smile. "I'm going to get blood on your nice clean blanket, Quinn."

"Let me worry about my blanket. I have a first aid kit in the car. Sit tight."

Quinn went outside and retrieved the kit from the

trunk of his Mercedes. On the way back he grabbed Molly's groceries, as well—those that could be salvaged. No point in giving the seagulls too extravagant a feast.

When he reentered the bedroom she looked a little pale, leaning on her right side, taking care not to let her messy abrasions come in contact with his blanket.

"Will you relax?" He sat next to her on the bed and urged her onto her back. "You know, you're really uptight, Molly. You should do something about that. Take a vacation or something."

He wondered if he'd ever seen anything as bewitching as her smirky little smile, knowing he'd put it there. Quinn opened the compact first aid kit and pawed through the various sealed packets. "Let's see…alcohol cleansing pads. I don't think so."

She leaned toward him to look. "What else do you have in there?"

"Iodine infection-control pads."

She wrinkled her nose. "Iodine? Doesn't that sting?"

He hated to break the news to her, but no matter what they used to clean those scrapes, it was bound to be a real attention getter. "Here we go." He lifted out a handful of packets. "Antiseptic cleansing wipes."

"That sounds promising."

Quinn tore open a packet and looked her over, trying to decide where to start. She tipped her head, indicating her chin. He unfolded the saturated wipe and touched it to the raw red abrasion.

She screamed and jumped back, slamming her skull into the wooden headboard.

"Okay." He grasped her forearm, firmly. "Okay, I know, but we have to clean these places—you know that, Molly. They'll get infected otherwise."

She squeezed her eyes shut and muttered a lot of words he wouldn't have thought she knew. Not Mellow Molly. He almost smiled.

"Okay. Ready?" he asked.

She nodded. He gingerly started cleaning her chin. She sucked in her breath and tensed, but didn't move.

"Next customer." Quinn eased the narrow strap of her tank top down over her scraped shoulder, knowing he wouldn't find a bra strap under it. In seven days of conscientious observation he had yet to detect a bra on Molly. She probably didn't own one. He opened another packet and applied it to the bloody open skin of her shoulder. A groan squeezed past her clamped jaw.

Distract her, he commanded himself. Before he could think of something to say, she asked, "How's the bike? I don't want to lose my deposit."

"You won't. I'll put the chain back on, realign the handlebars. No one'll notice another scratch or two."

Molly didn't own a car. Someone had given her a ride to the Cape and she'd rented the bicycle for local transportation.

He said, "I didn't know you were going to go grocery shopping with that thing. Why didn't you ask me for a lift?"

The instant the words were out of his mouth, he wanted to lop off his tongue. Molly avoided his eyes. They both knew the answer to that one. *No obligations, no distractions.*

"What I mean is, I have to go myself, anyway,

right?" he said. "No reason you can't tag along. I'll, uh, tell you next time I'm going to the supermarket."

He moved on to her abraded elbow. She looked away, and after an initial flinch, sat still and let him clean it. He admired her control. This had to hurt like hell.

"It's okay, Quinn," she said. "You don't have to take me shopping. I know you value your privacy. I do fine on the bike, I just got kinda carried away and tried to schlepp too much stuff home."

He fumbled for a response but came up empty. How could anyone be so damn easygoing? She ought to hate his guts for giving her the cold shoulder, for treating her friendly overtures like the onslaught of the Mongol hordes. Anyone else would have told him to take a flying leap the very first day, but not Molly.

Suddenly he knew why Phil had been attracted to her. Here was a woman he could lord it over, a woman who wouldn't challenge him or try to call the shots. He probably found her appealingly spineless.

Which wasn't a fair assessment of Molly. Quinn didn't think of her as spineless so much as…serene. There was something to be said for not letting things get to you. He wondered how she reacted in a crisis.

And what did his analysis say about Phil? Or rather, about his opinion of Phil? He'd be kidding himself if he said he actually liked the guy, and Quinn wasn't one to kid himself. But he didn't have to be pals with a man to respect him in business, to admire him even.

The bottom line was, something told Quinn that his former boss would appreciate a woman like Molly. More perplexing was what she'd seen in Phil.

Quinn wanted to ask her but didn't dare. How could he demand that his housemate respect his privacy if he didn't respect hers?

She asked, "Did my chicken cutlets survive?"

"Afraid not. The package split open. You lost the coleslaw, too. The hot dogs are okay, though. And the potato chip bag is flat but intact. Diet chips—you can eat just as many, but you won't get fat because they are now very, very tiny."

She watched him open one last packet to clean her knee, but again she averted her eyes just before he got down to business. He found that endearing somehow.

"I'm not up to barbecuing tonight anyway," she said. "I think I'll just open a can of tuna."

Quinn carefully dabbed the blood from her knee, chagrined at the internal battle he was waging. A battle between good common sense and...what? He didn't think he wanted to know. In the end the *what* won out.

"Well, if you don't mind lobster, you're welcome to eat down here," he said, his eyes still on his task. "With me."

She stared at him for long, agonizing moments. "Quinn, I know you don't want—"

"Just say yes, damn it!" He felt his face heating. "It's not like I'm some damn *hermit!*"

Her lips twitched. To her credit she refrained from saying something like *Well, yeah, Quinn, it is like you're some damn hermit.*

Instead she said, "Real lobster?"

"The fake ones are hell on the nutcrackers."

"I haven't had lobster in so long! Those chicken cutlets were my big splurge for the week."

"You can't leave the Cape without eating a lobster, Molly. There's some law on the books about it, if I'm not mistaken." He retrieved gauze pads, antibiotic ointment and a roll of adhesive tape from the first aid kit, uncomfortable with the sudden realization that if Molly didn't say yes, he wouldn't bother getting a lobster just for himself.

"What did I tell you?" she said, with a knowing look. "It's happening already. You're beginning to get it."

"Get what? You mean the whole beach-bumming, sunset-watching, bike-riding, lobster-sucking Cape Cod thing?"

"Exactly."

He peeled the paper wrapper from a gauze pad, squirted ointment on it and gently placed it on the scraped-up side of her chin. "Hold that for me." She did and he taped it in position. "You know, you're pretty cocky for someone angling for a free crustacean."

"With corn on the cob."

"Now she wants corn on the cob!" He unwrapped another piece of gauze.

"And steamers. A whole bucketful. You like clams?"

"No, but something tells me I won't want to miss a chance to watch you eat them."

"Lobster!" Molly squealed gleefully and bounced on the bed, derailing his attempt to bandage her elbow. She gave his thigh a brisk pat. "And after, we watch the sunset. The *whole* sunset."

4

"I TELL YOU, I don't see any damn swan." Quinn frowned up at the moonless heavens.

"You're trying too hard. Use your imagination."

"I don't have one."

Molly leaned on the second-floor deck railing next to Quinn, close enough to detect his warmth even through the sweatshirt she'd thrown over her tank top. A long-sleeved T-shirt was his only concession to the brisk evening breeze that carried the scents of the bay and the field of tall grasses that stretched between the house and the beach.

They were standing at the front end of the deck. The weathered boards were rough on the bare soles of Molly's feet. They'd turned off all the lights indoors, the better to see the stars. Overhead the night sky unfurled in all its majesty and mystery.

She said, "Don't try to focus on the image, just let it kind of…gel, you know?"

"Oh, that helps."

She smiled at his sarcastic tone. "Okay, you see the Milky Way, right?"

"Sure." He swept his left arm in a long arc, tracing the paler swath of indigo.

"Well, right in the middle of the Milky Way, right up there—" she pointed "—is Deneb, a blue supergiant, the brightest star in the constellation Cygnus. Latin for 'swan.'"

"Okay, I've got Deneb."

"Follow it straight down to the next star. And then out to both sides for the wings. And straight down for the body."

While he stared up at the sky, she stared at him, his profile strangely elegant and compelling by starlight. She wondered if he had the remotest inkling of his own raw physical appeal, and decided he probably didn't.

She'd been unprepared for the divergent feelings that had assailed her earlier when he'd carried her into his bedroom, nestled against his broad bare chest. There'd been the liberating, almost childlike sensation of surrendering yourself into the hands of another, knowing you'll be cared for, protected; and at the same time, the ever-present, almost exhausting awareness of *him.* Of smooth, sinewy, sun-gilded flesh. Of a deep, well-modulated voice custom-made for that surprising dry sense of humor. And the eyes…those dangerous eyes you couldn't look into for long because they were like rare cognac, or the finest sweet liqueur, enticing you to overindulge even as you felt your little brain cells popping one by one.

Molly took a deep, slow breath and forced her gaze back to the constellation. *Don't even think it*, she cautioned herself. *He's not interested.* And even if he were, the last thing she needed was another stuffy ad executive with a hidden agenda.

Okay, that wasn't fair. She didn't really know Quinn, after all. Didn't know about his agenda, hidden or otherwise, except that he was clearly a hard-driven workaholic, cast from the same mold as Phil Owen. Perhaps this was some sort of fatal attraction she was doomed to repeat over and over. Carefree copy editor meets anal-retentive ad man. Sparks fly. Hearts break.

"Give me a hint," Quinn groused. "What's this swan doing?" He rubbed the back of his neck.

"Doing? Oh. It's flying." She turned and spread her arms in demonstration. "It's a swan in flight."

Squinting up at the dome of stars, he started to shake his head, and froze. He blinked. "I see it. I think I see it!"

He spread his arms, too, and Molly thought how absurd the two of them must look, if anyone could see them, standing on the deck readying for takeoff. She placed a friendly hand on Quinn's back and felt the landscape of muscles shift under her palm as he lowered his arms.

"And you say you don't have an imagination!" she chided.

"Oh, sometimes I do."

His silky little smile steered her own overactive imagination into treacherous waters. She dropped her hand. "What's your sign?"

"What, my zodiac sign? Don't tell me you're into all that."

"I like to keep an open mind," she said, "but that's not why I asked. Maybe we can find your constellation."

"It's Cancer."

"Cancer. The Crab. Hey, your birthday's around now! When is it? Did it pass yet?"

He grinned.

"Not telling, huh? Well, I always enjoy a challenge." She looked up. "Unfortunately, we can't see the Crab in the summer. Have to wait till the fall and winter. I'm Taurus—we can't see the Bull tonight either."

He cocked his head. "The Bull, huh?"

She leaned back against the railing, not meeting his eyes. "I know what you're thinking. It fits. The way I bulled my way uninvited into your, you know, personal space and all."

After a moment he said quietly, "I don't think of it that way."

Why had she brought this up? "You're sweet to say so, Quinn, but it's all right. I know my personality can be a bit...overwhelming."

He braced his palm on the railing, right next to her. "Now, see, I wouldn't have put it like that. I would've said friendly. Openhearted."

A lopsided smile sprang to her lips despite her chagrin. "Openhearted. I like that one."

Was it her imagination, or did he edge closer? His scrumptious masculine scent invaded her nostrils, making her a little dizzy. "Outgoing yet serene," he continued. "Unflappable. Imperturbable."

"You can stop now."

"Insouciant."

"What?"

He laughed, the sound rich and warm and wonderfully spontaneous, and she realized it was the first time she'd heard him laugh. She was more than a little pleased to be the cause of it, even if he was having fun at her expense.

She said, "I've never been accused of insouciance before," and punched his chest in mock annoyance. He seized her wrist, surprising her with his speed and the leashed power she sensed beneath his gentle grip. His smile spread, his teeth gleaming in the dark, and now he was right there, standing over her, his breath stirring her hair, and she couldn't breathe, couldn't think because his nearness was crowding every blessed thought out of her head.

"You know, that was fun," he murmured, "watching you eat those steamers."

"I, um…" She cleared her throat. "I know I was a little messy."

"Now, see, I would've said provocative." His thumb traced circles on the inside of her wrist, and she shivered.

A nervous chuckle escaped her. "You say tomato, I say to*mah*to."

Slowly he brought her wrist up and pressed his lips to it, to the tender, tingling skin he'd just stroked. The stunning sensation rocketed along every nerve in her body. Molly gripped the railing hard with her other hand.

He said, "Thank you for letting me watch you eat steamers. Thank you for making me watch the sunset. Thank you for showing me the swan."

Her voice was a ragged whisper. "Thank you for fixing my boo-boos and buying me a two-pound lobster."

His black hair blended into the shadows, making his star-dusted face appear to float above her. "My pleasure," he said, and as she watched, his smile gradually faded. She sensed his natural reserve reasserting itself.

He's remembering, she thought. *Remembering who I am and what I did. Remembering how it felt to sit in a church pew waiting for a wedding that wasn't meant to be.*

He dropped her hand and stepped away.

Molly couldn't bear to hear him say it, so she said it herself. "It's getting late. I guess it's time to say good-night."

SHE'S BAKING, Quinn thought, closing the front door behind him and unlocking his part of the house. As always, the door at the top of the stairs stood wide open, and the ambrosial scent of something hot and sweet curled down the stairwell and tweaked his salivary glands.

It was close to nine, nearly dark, and he'd just returned from an excursion into town to pick up a couple of videotapes and a quart of butter pecan ice cream. He'd had little interaction with Molly during the five days since he'd fed her lobster and discovered a swan in the heavens, but neither had he gone to great lengths to avoid her as he had those first few days. Nevertheless, while his initial standoffishness had softened somewhat, a barrier stood between them, as insurmountable as the Berlin Wall before German unification.

This lady's past history spoke for itself; no amount of sugarcoating was going to put a palatable spin on what she'd done to Phil. The man under whose roof Quinn now dwelled. The man who boasted tremendous influence in Quinn's chosen profession.

Quinn had accepted Phil's offer of the house in part as a goodwill gesture, ever mindful of the folly of burning one's bridges. One never knew when someone from one's past might be in a position to help—or hinder—one's career. In Quinn's weaker moments, when he allowed himself to envision a sexy summer romp with his ex-boss's tantalizing ex-fiancée, images of a long vine-and-bamboo foot-bridge leaped to mind, awash in flames, breaking up in great blazing chunks and dropping into the fath-omless depths of a mist-shrouded gorge far, far be-low.

One thing he'd say for Molly, she'd given his long-dormant imagination a good kick in the butt.

He knew she sensed his continued aloofness. He saw it in the way she waited for him to initiate a con-versation, and how quick she was to end one, as if careful not to overstay her welcome. A few days ago he'd been relieved when she'd respected his desire to be left alone. Now all he felt was a sharp jab of shame.

Quinn had made his opinion of Molly excruciat-ingly clear. He'd condemned her actions—and by ex-tension, her character—to her face. His lingering ret-icence had to be painfully eloquent in her eyes.

It's not just that, he wanted to tell her. *It's my career, it's that bamboo footbridge I've spent eight long years building. I can't jeopardize all that by...*

By what? By being civil to her? There was a world of difference between treating someone like a pariah and asking her to have your baby. Maybe he ought to try for a middle ground.

Maybe he should have done that from the begin-ning.

Quinn made a beeline for the kitchen, tossing the videotapes on the coffee table without breaking stride. He set the sack from the ice cream shop on the counter and jumped at the sound of a knock at his door.

It could only be one person.

She stood in his doorway wearing an incandescent

smile and a short India-print sundress with skinny little shoulder straps. The scrapes from her bicycle accident had scabbed over nicely, but still looked like something out of a horror film. It took him a moment to register what she held in her hands.

"Happy birthday!" she shouted.

It walloped him like a two-by-four, and all he could do was stand there staring stupidly at the chocolate birthday cake. Melting wax dripped down lit candles shaped like the numbers 3 and 0.

After a few moments Molly's smile began to falter. Quinn swallowed hard. He tried to force this remarkable event into some compartment of his brain that would recognize it. Categorize it.

It refused to fit.

"Um, can I come in?" she asked. "I just wanted to, you know, drop this off."

"You made me a cake." Was that his voice, so flat? "Why did you do this?"

Quinn watched dismay chase the last vestiges of her smile, jerking him out of his stupor at last.

"I mean—" His voice cracked. "Molly. No one's ever made me a birthday cake." Even his mother used to order them from the bakery.

He stared into her blue-violet eyes and she stared back, and something arced between them that stung his eyes and closed his throat, and damn it, he had to pull himself together fast.

With a gentle smile she said, "Then it's about time, isn't it?" and he knew she saw it all, saw his struggle and his raw open soul, saw the wonder and bafflement he couldn't hide, and it was okay.

This was Molly and it was okay.

He exhaled a fierce breath as if he'd run a race. He

smiled and reached for the cake plate, knowing his hands were trembling, and not really caring if she noticed. "Wow. This is so... Is that a circus train?"

The cake was a bit lopsided, slathered in chocolate butter cream. A jittery Happy Birthday Quinn had been lovingly executed in yellow icing by someone presumably in the throes of the d.t.'s. The candles were burning low and listing in opposite directions. And along the perimeter was a tiny, colorful candy train, complete with cagelike boxcars occupied by grinning circus animals.

Molly adjusted the caboose. "Yes, it is. They had a limited selection at the Pay and Weep," she said, referring to the local convenience store, Park and Shop. "It was either this or clowns."

"Thank you. A choo-choo train is much more dignified."

"Blow out the candles. Oh! Make a wish first!"

He felt an absurd kind of panic for an instant— what should he wish for? Then he smiled at his idiocy and closed his eyes and made a wish. A modest wish as birthday wishes went, with no dollar signs attached. He blew out the candles.

She fiddled with her hair. "It's not from scratch. I used, you know, a mix."

"It's...it's perfect, Molly. I smelled it coming in and wondered what you were baking."

"I'm not very artistic." She gestured to the wobbly words inscribed on the cake. "The writing—"

"I love the writing. I love the whole thing." He stepped back to allow her to enter. "Listen, come in. Let me get a couple of plates."

She took a few tentative steps inside as he carried

the cake into the kitchen. She said, "I really only meant to drop it off. You don't have to—"

"I have ice cream, too," he called. "Butter pecan. This is shaping up to be a regular birthday party. Did you pick up any of those little Cone Head hats?"

She appeared in the arched entrance to the kitchen, looking more beautiful than he'd ever seen her, with her long, sun-streaked hair loose around her bare shoulders, and wearing a tender, almost shy little smile. She shook her head at his question.

He dragged two small plates out of a cupboard. "Noisemakers?"

She shook her head again, her smile growing.

He sighed in mock disappointment. "I don't know, Molly. What kind of a party are we talking about here? No noisemakers. No Pin-the-tail-on-the-donkey." He drew the carton of ice cream out of the bag and pulled off the lid.

Grinning now, Molly leaned her shoulder against the archway. Her folded arms pushed up her breasts just enough to make spectacular things happen in the V neck of her dress.

Quinn had seen her stark naked, so why did the sight of a little cleavage suddenly turn him stupid? He strained to recall what he'd been doing. Forks. Right. Spoons, bowls, napkins.

"Coffee?" he asked.

"Too late for me. Do you have decaf?"

"Sorry, just high-test."

"Aren't you afraid it'll keep you up all night?"

In his current frame of mind, being "up" all night was not an entirely unwelcome prospect. Not if his housemate was somewhere in the equation.

"Never bothers me," he said, "but I won't brew a

pot if it's just for me. Why don't you cut the cake while I put on some party music."

"I vote for the Supremes."

A few minutes later he was tucking into the huge slab of cake Molly had served him. They sat across from each other at the plastic-draped dining table listening to Diana Ross and company warn them to stop! in the name of love. "So I give up," he said. "How did you find out it's my birthday?"

"I called Cindy at the agency."

"Cindy? Oh, the office manager."

"She checked your personnel file and gave me your date of birth. Thirty! That's a very important milestone, Quinn. It deserves to be celebrated."

He thought about that. "If anything deserves to be celebrated, it's the fact that I attained the goals I set for myself—the things I wanted to accomplish by age thirty." He grimaced. "My current employment status notwithstanding."

"So by goals, you mean career goals."

He shrugged. "You achieve those, the rest falls into place."

"The rest being…"

"You have to ask? Money. Filthy lucre. And all the stuff it gets you."

"That's the material side," she said. "What about personal goals?"

"It's all related. When you've achieved a certain status in your chosen profession, the rest follows, like I said. Including the respect and esteem of others."

Molly licked her ice cream spoon clean. "So…the higher your professional status, the more money you make, the more friends you have?"

He said, "You have ice cream on your nose," and watched her impish smile disappear as she glanced at her nose cross-eyed. Her tongue flicked out in a futile attempt to lick off the ice cream, and Quinn's body responded as though she'd found the on-off switch.

Shrugging good-naturedly, she resorted to the prosaic solution of a paper napkin, but the damage had been done. The image of that supple pink tongue, straining with single-minded intent, had found a permanent home in the brain wrinkle occupied by tenacious TV commercial jingles and Embarrassing Moments. He'd carry it to the grave.

Quinn pushed away his plate and leaned back in his chair. "I'm going to ask you something," he said, pretty certain he'd regret it.

Then again, maybe not. This wasn't the shallow, uncomplicated Molly he thought he'd met nearly two weeks ago. This wasn't the heartless Molly whom Phil had described to him in unloving detail. That woman wouldn't have shrugged off Quinn's insulting brush-offs day after day. She wouldn't have given him a tour of the night sky with saintlike patience. She certainly wouldn't have gone to the trouble of ferreting out his birthday and making him a cake.

She'd made him a cake. He still couldn't get over it. The bigness of her heart and her unreserved joie de vivre left him in awe.

She propped her elbows on the table, then rested her chin on her laced fingers, waiting.

He asked, "Why did you walk out on your wedding?"

5

SHE JUST STARED AT HIM for the longest time, and he braced himself for anything from tears to hilarity. Finally she sat up, dropped her hands into her lap and smiled wanly. "When I tell you, you might still see things Phil's way. It's not exactly a black-and-white issue."

"Not much in life is. What happened? You were at the church," he prompted. "In your Cinderella gown."

She took a deep breath. "I was waiting in the room set aside for the bride. Nervous, you know. Happy but nervous. Like all brides, I guess. My sister Toni was with me. She was my matron of honor. It was time for the wedding to start and Phil knocked on the door. I didn't want him to, you know, see the dress beforehand, but he said it was important and he came in with his brother Ron and this friend of his, Jim."

"What did he want?"

"A last-minute detail, he said, something that had to be taken care of before we could get married. He handed me this document to sign. It was a contract, all legal. He didn't use the words *prenuptial agreement*, he called it an 'understanding.'"

"Wait a minute." Quinn sat up straight. "He presents you with a prenup right when you're about to walk down the aisle?"

She nodded. "He said it was his lawyer's idea, that if it was up to him, he wouldn't bother, but his lawyer was real insistent. Ron and Jim were there to witness our signatures. I asked Phil why he hadn't shown this to me before. He said there were these unavoidable delays and his lawyer had just given him the paperwork that morning right there at the church. I didn't know what to make of this story, so I turned to his brother."

"The guy who taught you to bluff in poker."

"Right. Ron was my friend. A decent guy. Anyway, I know what his poker face looks like and I saw it then—I saw him making this heroic effort to support his brother. But as I stared at him, really made him look me in the eye, he gave it up and kind of looked away, ashamed. That's when—"

Her voice broke, and a jolt of alarm shot through Quinn. He'd never seen her anything but unflappable.

She said hoarsely, "That's when I knew Phil was lying. Shoving that contract in my face at the very last minute was a calculated tactic. He thought I'd cave in and sign it. I mean, the church was packed, I could hear the guests in the sanctuary, the organ music. We had this whole huge reception planned and paid for, honeymoon reservations, the works." Molly's lower lip trembled, though her words were spoken calmly.

Quinn asked gently, "What did you do?"

"I told Phil I couldn't possibly sign a contract like that without having a lawyer look at it. And no, I didn't happen to have one there at the church like he did. He said there was no time, it had to be signed before we could get married."

"What were the terms of the contract?" As if he couldn't guess.

"It was totally in his favor—big surprise. If we divorced, even if it was after something like forty years, I'd walk away only with whatever I brought into the marriage. Which is, like, my toothbrush, right? I wouldn't have been entitled to any assets accumulated during the marriage, since he was going to be the breadwinner."

"You weren't going to work, then?"

"Not outside the home. Phil and I wanted to start a family right away, and we both agreed I should stay home and raise the kids, manage the house and all that—which, let me tell you, is just as important a contribution to the family unit as his income. But if we divorced, under his contract my years of hard work would count for nothing."

"No lawyer would let you sign a one-sided contract like that, Molly."

"Phil got kind of nasty when I balked. I guess he thought I'd knuckle under right away. I mean, I know I'm easygoing, but let's get real!"

Quinn chewed back a grin. He'd wondered how Molly would react in a crisis. It appeared he'd just found out.

She said, "That's when he dropped all the pretense and said sign it now or the wedding's off."

"And you walked." Admiration for Molly swelled within him like a balloon.

"I asked Toni for the keys to her car, asked her to stay and explain the whole thing to Mom and Dad. Then I just turned around and walked out the back way, head held high and all that." She added proudly, "He never saw me shed a tear."

Which didn't mean there hadn't been plenty of them, Quinn guessed, watching her blink back the glaze of moisture in her eyes. He was beginning to realize Phil's treachery affected her more deeply than she wanted to let on, even to herself. At the same time Quinn marveled at the inner strength and self-respect that had allowed her to stand up to the son of a bitch.

Just chock-full of surprises, his Mellow Molly.

"Why did you say that," he asked, "about how I might still see things Phil's way once I heard your story? I'm not sure how to take that."

"I only meant, you know, since the two of you have so much in common." She brought the candy locomotive to her mouth and sucked off the frosting that clung to it.

"Wait a minute." Quinn made a "time-out" T with his hands. "We have so much in common? Me and that...that—"

"No offense," she said.

"No offense! Would you care to elaborate?"

Molly obligingly ticked off the similarities on her fingers. "You're both in advertising. Both go-getters. Successful. Ambitious. Material interests are everything." She started on her other hand. "Nothing stands in the way of your goals. Personal relationships are an extension of your professional life. Dark hair. German car. Swell shoulders." She wiggled her ten fingers. "My calculator's run out of batteries. Oh yeah, you wear the same vacation uniform. Polo shirts and khakis. Very dress-down Friday."

"Well, that's—that's just great!" Quinn sputtered.

"Do you disagree with any of that?" She reached across the table to paw through the debris on his plate. "Where's the caboose? Did you eat it?"

"Can you stick to one subject at a time? No, I don't disagree with your comparison, as far as it goes, but there's a lot more to me than material interests and...and—" *swell shoulders* "—my Mercedes. I'd never do to any woman what Phil did to you!"

"Oh, I know that, Quinn. Gosh. I don't think you guys are clones or anything."

"Well, all right."

"You'd give your bride plenty of time to look over the prenup."

He would? Was he the kind of guy to insist on a prenuptial agreement if he married a woman of significantly lesser means? Molly seemed to think so. The hell of it was, she was probably right. Even so, Quinn would never try to cheat his intended out of her fair share of the marital assets.

Phil had freely invited Quinn to spend an entire month under the same roof with his wronged ex-fiancée. Hadn't he been concerned that they'd talk about him, that Quinn would learn what Phil had done to her?

Probably not. Phil only knew him from the agency, after all, where Quinn's demeanor had been all business. No doubt Phil assumed that the hard-boiled corporate persona was an accurate reflection of the private man—which, in the case of Phil himself, was obviously true. Then, too, having regaled Quinn with horror tales of his unprincipled ex, Phil must have counted on him giving Molly a wide berth.

Which he had, indeed, made every attempt to do. Quinn wasn't proud of that.

He asked, "Phil's got swell shoulders?"

"Yours are sweller."

"Thank you."

"His BMW's bigger, though. More horsepower. More leather."

"Well, Phil and I might be two peas in a damn pod," Quinn said, "but just for the record, I'm appalled by the stunt he tried to pull on you. I can't believe you aren't bitter. I mean out-for-blood, hell-hath-no-fury bitter. Do you have any idea what Phil's been saying about you, the vicious office gossip?"

"I can imagine. It's not important. No one with half a brain and even the tiniest scrap of sensitivity would take Phil's version of events at face value."

Quinn tried not to squirm. Wasn't that precisely what he'd done? And he hadn't even shown Molly the courtesy of listening to her explanation back when she'd first tried to give it.

His thoughts must have been evident. She reached across the table and squeezed his hand. "I didn't mean you, Quinn. You didn't know me then."

He shook his head in wonder. "You're too good, you know that? Too understanding, too…sweet. If it had been me, if someone had done to me what Phil did to you, I'd take out a full-page ad in the *New York Times* and share it with the world. No, I've got it. An open letter in *Advertising Today*!"

She laughed. "Remind me never to cross you."

"How can you not hold a grudge?"

She shrugged. "Phil did what he had to do. What his gut—his self-preservation instincts, I guess—told him to do. It's how he got where he is today, owner of a multimillion-dollar ad agency."

"That's business! That's not the way you're supposed to treat people you care about."

She smiled knowingly. "I thought it was all related. Isn't that what you said?"

Quinn slumped in his chair. "That's not what I meant."

"He runs his private life the way he runs his business. See, that's something I didn't realize before the wedding."

"There you go again, sounding so damn sanguine about the whole thing."

She shrugged. "Phil did what he had to do and I did what I had to do. No hard feelings."

"Bull." He made her meet his eyes. "You're hurt, Molly. You gonna try to deny it?"

"No," she said quietly. "But I'll get over it. I've mostly put it behind me. I mean, what's the use of letting myself wallow in bitterness and hatred? That just eats you up from the inside. Then you're punishing yourself, not the person who hurt you."

"Please don't tell me you've forgiven him."

Her beatific smile said it all.

"Oh, Molly," he groaned.

"Now, don't get yourself all worked up. Don't start doing my hating for me."

Somebody had to do it! He debated with himself for a whole two seconds before blurting, "You may not hold a grudge, but Phil sure does."

She scraped her cake plate clean with her fork. "I know. He's saying terrible things about me."

"He's doing more than that, and you're letting him. Damn it, Molly!"

Her eyes widened at his harsh tone. "What did I do?"

"You can't really believe nine-fifty a week is a bargain for this place?"

She stared, unblinking, and he saw his words register, saw the inevitable and unwelcome conclusion latch on with sharp little claws. Watching her expressive face, Quinn had to give Phil's brother credit for trying, but no one was ever going to teach this woman to bluff.

Quinn's motives had been pure. If she was determined to play Saint Molly, the least he could do was arm her with all the facts. That was what he'd told himself, but what he saw on her face made him wish he'd kept his mouth shut.

She made a valiant effort to smile. "Well. I guess I bungled that one, huh? Think he's having a good laugh right about now?"

"Molly…" Quinn said miserably. "I'm sorry, I shouldn't have—"

"Don't be silly. I'm glad you did." She sat up straighter, her dignified speech and posture at odds with the twin spots of color in her tanned cheeks, and a hard glitter in her eyes he'd never seen before. "Do you mind if I ask what you're paying?"

You started this, he chided himself. *Why stop now when she has a scrap of self-esteem left?* "I'm…I'm not paying anything, Molly. He, uh, offered me the place free."

One delicate eyebrow lifted slightly, as if this were of passing interest. He almost expected to hear, "How nice for you."

He made himself continue. "I think he's charging you a couple of hundred a week more than he usually gets—there's plenty of competition from places in a lot better shape."

"Thank you for telling me this, Quinn."

Molly stood and quickly gathered the dishes, then carried them into the kitchen. He heard plates and flatwear clatter into the sink, heard the faucet open full blast.

Quinn cursed under his breath. He'd offer to pay her rent himself if he thought she'd accept it. But the money itself wasn't the issue, he knew.

He sat listening to the amplified *scritch scritch scritch* of the phonograph needle gnawing on vinyl, until it finally dawned on him that the machine didn't know the music had ended. He went into the living room, switched it off and lifted the record from the turntable.

In the sudden quiet a soft sound came to his ears, barely audible. Muffled weeping. He tossed the record aside and hurried into the kitchen.

Molly stood at the sink squirting an endless stream of liquid soap into the rising water. Quinn didn't think she was aware of the spuming foam threatening to overflow onto the floor. Her chin wobbled and tears welled in her eyes. He turned off the water and took the detergent bottle from her.

"He had to have the last laugh." She pounded the worn countertop with her fist. "His first try at cheating me didn't work, so he had to have another stab at it. And I just *let* him because I'm so *ditsy!*" The tears spilled down her cheeks.

"Molly, you're not—"

"I'm a *doormat!* Even after what he tried to do, I *trusted* him. I mean, I walked right *into* it!" She gestured wildly, and shook off the comforting hand Quinn laid on her back.

He said, "If you were a doormat, you would have

walked down the aisle with Phil because you'd have been too timid or embarrassed to call it off at the last minute. If you trusted him about the rent, it's because you see the good in people. And it's that goodness you concentrate on, not the person's faults. You bring out the best in people, Molly."

She leaned back against the refrigerator, hugging herself. "Like I brought out the best in Phil?"

"You can't bring out what's not there to begin with. You're blaming yourself for this when you should be blaming him. You're doing what you just talked about—punishing yourself, instead of the person who hurt you."

"He—he used to be so sweet, Quinn. When we were together. Devoted. I mean, I know now it was an act."

Quinn edged closer and tipped her face up, so she'd be forced to see his sincerity. She tried to turn away, but he wouldn't let her. "You saw the good in me," he said. "You ignored my many loathsome faults and focused on my pitifully few virtues, and look at me now." He smiled down into her sullen, watery eyes. "When that sun sets, I'm the first guy on the beach and the last one to leave. King of the Cape, they call me."

She pushed ineffectually at his chest. "You're just trying to make me feel better."

"Well, there you go! Could you see me doing that two weeks ago?" He grabbed a paper napkin from the counter and blotted her tears. She took it from him, dabbed at her nose and lobbed it into the corner garbage can.

Her fragrance heightened his awareness of how close they stood—not a store-bought perfume but her own subtle, alluring scent. He ignored the cautionary voice inside his head and moved closer still, leaning both forearms on the refrigerator door to corral her.

Molly glanced up into his eyes, and he saw the answering awareness she couldn't hide, felt it reach deep inside and tug at the most primitive part of him. She averted her face. Her chest rose and fell in a quickened rhythm and he leaned into her until her soft breasts nudged him with each breath.

Quinn lowered his mouth to her throat, seeking her pulse, the hot rush of life there. Her breath caught and her hands came up, fluttering, uncertain. To hold him or to push him away? Did she know?

His lips nuzzled her. The breathless little sounds she made inflamed him. He felt her fighting it, felt her resisting this thing that had been brewing between them for nearly two weeks, and this excited him, challenged the primal male animal she'd awakened.

"Molly..." he breathed against her throat. She shuddered. His fingers were threaded into her hair, holding her, and he didn't know how they'd gotten there. He was acting on instinct and it felt damn good.

His other hand caressed her waist, her hip, slowly, cajolingly. It glided up her rib cage. He heard and felt her soft, panting breaths, felt her rising excitement, and perhaps a touch of panic. The heavy warmth of her breast nestled in the crook of his hand; his thumb lightly stroked the underswell. Her fingernails bit into his shoulders as she struggled to fend off not him, he sensed, but her own mounting desire.

He sought the truth in her expressive face. Her

eyes had that drowsy, needy look; her mouth was slightly parted, her skin flushed.

Quinn pounced in unthinking reflex, seizing her mouth in a hard kiss, crushing her against the refrigerator. This kiss was thorough, unashamedly possessive; it demanded a response. And still Molly held back. He intensified the siege, angling his head, shifting his body to fit her pliant curves.

He nibbled at her closed lips, licked the seam. "Molly," he whispered, "stop fighting it, you won't win."

He captured her buttocks and pulled her closer still. Her mouth opened on a gasp and he took advantage, plying her with short, coaxing strokes of his tongue, more a stealthy infiltration than an invasion.

Quinn knew his patience had been rewarded when he heard her soft moan. She melted a little, opened to him, surrendering at last. Triumph surged hard and hot within him. His hands covered her breasts. Their stiff peaks teased his palms and he brushed them lightly, teasing her in return, inhaling the helpless whimpers that rose in her throat.

He relinquished her mouth and gazed at her, the picture of earthy sensuality, panting softly, eyes half-closed, nipples jutting under the flimsy fabric of her dress. In that instant his sanity hinged on getting her out of her clothes and into his bed. Now.

His hand slid under the short hem of her skirt and up her thigh, which was even silkier than he'd imagined. And he'd imagined it a lot in the past twelve days. He nudged her legs apart with his knee and continued the exploration. While Molly eschewed a bra, she did, he now discovered, wear underpants.

Practical cotton, by the feel of them, but skimpy. Not much to them.

His fingers slipped between her legs, probing, seeking, and he felt the melting heat of her passion right through the thin cotton. She stared up at him, dazed with that passion. Her trembling legs parted farther as if of their own volition.

She whispered, "Can we make it to your bedroom?"

Quinn pressed himself into the cradle of her hips, so there'd be no mistaking his state of readiness. "I'm thinking that countertop looks pretty good."

She chuckled. "I'd say go for it, but something tells me you don't keep condoms in here with the Frosted Flakes."

Red alert! his mind screamed. He forced himself to admit, "Uh, Molly honey, I don't have any condoms."

No distractions—that was the whole idea of this trip, wasn't it? You don't pack Trojans when you're planning on no distractions.

He said, "I suppose it's too much to hope you have some upstairs?"

She shook her head.

And the drugstore was closed at that late hour. If there was one thing Quinn had learned in eight years in the ad business, it was how to salvage a foundering presentation. He said, "You know, I've recently discovered that I can be exceptionally imaginative. One might even say inventive."

A slow smile touched her face. "Is that so?"

"Yes it is, and I'd be privileged to demonstrate this newfound inventiveness, at no risk to you whatsoever."

Molly wrapped her arms around his neck. "Well. I must admit I'm…intrigued."

He lifted her by the hips and spun around to set her on the counter, shoving aside the cake plate and upsetting the sugar bowl. He kissed her hungrily and pushed up her dress.

She wriggled to help him as he worked her underpants over her hips. "I've been trying not to let myself even *think* about you this way," she said.

"Me, too." He pulled the underpants down her legs and over her sandaled feet, and tossed them on the toaster. "But let's face it, Phil doesn't ever have to find out."

"Phil? What does this have to do with Phil?"

Quinn tried to part Molly's legs, but she locked her knees together. She pushed her skirt firmly into her lap and placed a staying hand on his shoulder when he went for another kiss. "Quinn? What's this about Phil?"

"Only that we have to keep this from him. Come on, Molly, I don't have to spell it out for you, do I?"

"Maybe you do."

He backed off a little and studied her expression. Wariness had replaced the glaze of desire in her eyes. He said, "Phil is a force to be reckoned with in my industry. You know that. He's in a position to either help or hurt me. Big time. If he got wind of this…" Quinn gestured to the two of them, and the promise of imminent debauchery.

Molly's morose little head shake told him debauchery was no longer imminent. As if to herself, she muttered, "I should've listened to my gut. I knew this was a mistake." She grabbed her underpants and stuck her feet into them. She hopped down from the counter and pulled the pants up, all in one efficient motion.

"Molly, what's with you?" He followed her into the living room.

"It's getting a little crowded in here, Quinn. You. Me. The force to be reckoned with." She opened the door.

"Don't you think you're overreacting?"

She turned to him with a pensive expression, clearly giving his question serious thought. "Perhaps," she said pleasantly, "but I don't like secrets. I'm not going to hide what I do as if it's something shameful. I understand your preoccupation with business, with your career, and that's okay. That's you."

"Oh, for pity's sake."

"The bottom line is this. Phil stopped being part of my love life four months ago, and that's the way I want to keep it." She rose on tiptoe and kissed his cheek, with a wistful little smile. "Happy birthday, Quinn. I hope your wish comes true." Then she was gone, her footfalls receding up the stairs.

He said, "It didn't."

6

MOLLY HAD EXPECTED the rain to let up by midday, but if anything, it had only gotten heavier, and now the wind had picked up as well. She stood before the sliding door that opened onto the deck, watching the expanse of tall grasses between the house and the beach ripple and sway under the onslaught. White-caps studded the bay. The sky grew darker by the minute.

Well, she couldn't complain; they'd had twenty-six days of near perfect weather. Molly smiled. When had she started thinking of this vacation in terms of "they"? And had Quinn slipped into the same mind-set?

Probably. The past two weeks since his birthday had been far different from those first strained days. They now shared the house in a natural, relaxed way. By unspoken agreement, they had the run of each other's space, with no locked doors between them.

Most meals were joint ventures. One beach blanket served the two of them. Together they dined in the local seafood restaurants, perused the gift and an-tiques stores, and occasionally, when the docile bay seemed too boring, they crossed the Cape for the pugnacious waves of the Atlantic. Quinn had even rented a bike to accompany Molly on two-wheeled tours of the surrounding area.

They'd gone out to the movies a couple of nights, to take in the latest crop of summer action flicks. And when Molly had discovered Quinn had never bowled, she'd dragged him whining and moping to the nearest alley. He'd made no secret of the fact he considered bowling a lowbrow pseudosport for bored housewives and middle-aged guys with prodigious beer guts and no discernible athletic skills—which made his initiation all the more humbling.

Molly had assured him her score of 202 was a fluke; her average was a mere 187. She'd almost regretted taking him when he refused to leave until he'd elevated his score into the three digits. They'd returned a few times and he'd shown rapid improvement. He now talked of perfecting his technique through books and videos, and investing in the best-quality ball, bag and shoes.

Most evenings, however, they stayed in, playing poker, watching videos or simply listening to music and talking. Sometimes Molly accompanied the old records on her trumpet, at Quinn's urging. This gave him the opening to launch into off-color observations regarding female horn players, until she was laughing too hard to continue.

One recent evening she'd employed her feminine wiles and most of a blender of slushy, sneakily strong margaritas to persuade him to dance with her. It might have been the tequila, but Quinn did the old rock tunes justice, with sexy, loose-jointed moves and a surprisingly sound sense of rhythm.

Molly couldn't kid herself: they weren't just friends. Their relationship had passed the point of simple friendship when they came close to doing the wild thing on Quinn's kitchen counter. She hadn't allowed things to get that out of hand since.

She meant what she'd told Quinn. Yes, she understood his concerns regarding his career, but she had no intention of sneaking around, and she especially had no intention of sneaking around behind her ex-fiancé's back, of all people. The usurious rent he'd charged her had been a painful and expensive lesson. But not a wasted one. Phil Owen was now officially out of her life. She refused to allow him even unwitting control over any aspect of it. And that included being forced to treat the act of love like some sordid little secret.

And Quinn still insisted on secrecy, even though he now had even more reason to despise Phil. He'd told Molly that he'd believed Phil's explanation for letting him go, that the merger with Glacken and Ross had created circumstances beyond his control. However, after Molly's bombshell revelation about the prenuptial agreement, Quinn began to examine the events leading up to his firing.

The day after his birthday, he'd made a few discreet phone calls and got the inside scoop: the guy brought in to replace him was a close relative of Phil's. Quinn's job should have been secure, merger or no merger. After that, it wasn't hard to deduce that free use of the beach house was a placating gesture in case Quinn ever managed to discover he'd lost his job to nepotism.

Quinn freely acknowledged that this latest disclosure only bolstered his disgust of his former boss. Nevertheless, Phil was still a Force to Be Reckoned With. In light of a recent day trip Molly had made to

Nantucket, Quinn's worries were probably moot, but she wouldn't share that with him just yet. Call her selfish, but she needed to know where she stood with him. If she didn't mean enough to him that he'd risk Phil's wrath, perhaps theirs was meant to be only a shallow and sexless summer fling. And in five days they'd go their separate ways.

But their differences went beyond his fixation on secrecy. She was terrified of repeating her previous disastrous mistake. No, Quinn and Phil weren't clones, but the similarities were undeniable. Quinn argued that they were also superficial, and the more she got to know him, the more she had to agree. Still, hadn't Phil been Mr. Right not so long ago? In the words of the old adage, fool me twice, shame on me.

She'd lost her head with Quinn once; ever since, she'd been on her guard, determined to avoid a repeat performance. Thus their displays of affection were tame by most couples' standards. Such as the little gifts they exchanged—sometimes silly, sometimes sentimental, anything that caught their fancy or reminded one of the other. From him, a tiny scrimshaw charm on a neck chain, inscribed with the image of a swan. From her, a plush stuffed crab, souvenir of Cape Cod, in honor of his zodiac sign.

Molly gave Quinn long, pampering back rubs. He brushed her hair until she moaned in pure hedonistic bliss. They necked on the beach, more playful than passionate. In the house they freely touched and kissed and cuddled, but she always reined in the action well before the point of no return. It wasn't easy. Quinn employed an impressive array of seduction skills in an effort to tip the scales. He still wanted to make love to her, but on his own terms—as a strictly clandestine liaison. She tried not to let on how much sheer grit it took to resist him.

Her gaze was focused on the distant horizon, now murky and indistinct, when a dark figure appeared out of nowhere and rapped sharply on the glass of the sliding door.

Molly jumped with a shriek. In the next heartbeat she recognized the man standing on the deck in the downpour. Quinn pointed to the door latch. "Open up."

She unlocked it and tried to pull it open, but this was one of the doors that didn't want to budge. Quinn added his brawn to the effort and the door jerked about two feet along its track, squealing in protest. He stepped inside and muscled it closed.

In the gloom of the rain-hued afternoon his smiling eyes seem to glow like gray-green gems in his tanned face—those heavy-lidded gigolo eyes that no longer seemed so incongruous, now that she'd experienced the sensual side of this man she'd once thought of in such one-dimensional terms.

"You're drenched!" she said.

He glanced at the puddle gathering on the tile floor at his feet. His black polo shirt and olive drab chinos clung to his body. He swept his fingers through his sodden hair and it stood up in black spikes.

He looked too delicious to resist, and Molly didn't even try. She stretched on tiptoes for what she intended as a quick kiss, but for some reason the feel of his lips, rain wet and chilly, the light rasp of afternoon whiskers, roused something within her, something with a mind of its own. She kissed him greedily, making little yummy noises. A low, feral sound rumbled up his throat as he began to respond.

She switched gears abruptly and licked his lips, with ravenous cat laps, the rain and Quinn both sweet on her tongue. After a bark of surprise, he made a grab for her, but she was ready with an evasive maneuver, laughing, getting in a few more haphazard swipes of her tongue before he caught her.

Quinn clamped his arms around Molly, pressing her to his soaking wet clothes. A wicked chuckle bubbled against her mouth as he took charge of the kiss. She wriggled and squirmed in a futile attempt to escape, but he only held her tighter. At last he released her and she staggered back a step, laughing breathlessly, her lips buzzing.

"There!" he said with a triumphant grin. "Don't mess with *me*, sister!"

"You got me wet!"

"Really?" he asked, a study in male impudence.

I'm getting there, she could have answered, but offered only an exasperated smirk.

His intense gaze homed in on her torso. She followed his line of sight, almost expecting to see twin gray-green laser beams. Her pale blue T-shirt, now thoroughly wet and practically transparent, was plastered to her breasts. Her nipples rose in dusky points.

Of course, he'd seen her buck naked, but there was nothing like a teasing glimpse to light a guy's fire. What strange and curious creatures men were, she thought. But lovable, by and large. And a surprising number of them smelled good and moved heavy objects without complaint. Even the debacle with Phil hadn't soured Molly on the male of the species.

She plucked the shirt from her skin. When she released it, it clung once more. She asked, "Didn't your mother ever teach you to come in out of the rain?"

"I thought that's what I just did."

"What were you doing out there?"

"Bringing all the lawn furniture into the house. I already did the first floor." At her quizzical look he said, "Hurricane's on the way, Molly."

"No!"

"Didn't you hear it on the news?"

"TV's been off all day. Aren't we supposed to evacuate or something? Run like heck away from the coast?"

"It's not going to be that bad," he said. "We should be fine if we just batten down the hatches."

"What can I do?"

"Well, there was this public health warning. If you're wearing a wet T-shirt, it has to come off. Immediately."

"Nice try."

"Suit yourself, but don't blame me if you catch, uh, hurricane fever."

"Aren't we supposed to, like, nail wood over the windows or something?" she asked.

"Ideally, but if you think I'm going to jump in my car and hunt for a lumberyard and bust my butt to secure a house whose owner is letting it fall apart anyway, think again."

"You've got a point."

"Actually, I have some duct tape in my car. We'll tape all the windows and doors so at least if one breaks, it won't shatter all over." He nodded toward her deck. "Speaking of which, I've got to bring all your stuff inside or it could come flying through the glass later. Why don't you put some water in pots, pitchers, whatever you can find, in case the water supply becomes contaminated? And see if you can scare up some candles—we could lose power."

"Good idea. Ooh, this is exciting!"

Quinn smiled at her enthusiasm and pulled the sliding door open. Wind-driven rain blew in and pelted him. He adopted a W. C. Fields twang, fresh in Molly's mind from last night's Fields movie marathon. "'Tain't a fit night out for man nor beast! I'm going out to milk the elk, dear."

While he moved her picnic table, chairs and grill inside, Molly changed into a tie-dyed halter top and green sweat shorts with a rolled-up hem. She filled all available vessels with water and ransacked the closets, earning only a smelly citronella candle and a flashlight with dead batteries for her efforts.

Quinn had piled up the lawn furniture in a corner of the living room. He started pulling off his sodden clothes on his way downstairs, and returned a few minutes later in dry shorts and a T-shirt Molly had bought for him at the local army-navy store, in hopes of weaning him away from his stuffy "vacation uniform." The shirt was gray with a design that hearkened back to the World War II navy construction battalions, the Seabees: a cartoon bumblebee wearing a fierce expression and a navy cap, holding tools and firing a weapon.

Quinn had retrieved the duct tape from his car, as well as a hefty, macho-looking flashlight that worked. In addition, he'd located a nearly full box of four dozen white utility candles under the kitchen sink.

Meanwhile Molly had cleared a space in the living

room and thrown a thick quilt and a couple of sofa cushions on the floor as a sort of cozy nest from which to observe Mother Nature's shenanigans. Their view was impeded only by the crisscrossing strips of duct tape Quinn now placed on the glass of the sliding door. Within minutes all the glass in the house was similarly adorned.

"There." He tossed the leftover tape onto a lamp table. "We've done what we can."

"Join me." Molly patted the quilt next to her. Sitting cross-legged, facing the sliding door and the rapidly escalating storm, she twisted a corkscrew into a bottle of burgundy and worked the cork out. She poured wine into two juice glasses.

Quinn kicked off his deck shoes and settled next to her on the quilt. He accepted a glass. "I should've known you'd find a way to turn a hurricane into high entertainment."

"You know, we should turn off all the lights, get a better view."

As if on command, the lights flickered for a few moments. Molly giggled. She waved her arms imperiously. "Forces of darkness, hear my command!"

The lights blinked out and Molly shot her fist in the air. "Yes! I have the power!"

Quinn set his glass aside and came to his feet. He offered Molly his hand. "If the high priestess of the dark forces isn't above lighting a few candles, I could use some help."

In short order they had a dozen lit utility candles arranged around the room, using coffee mugs and small plates for candleholders. Outside it was now nearly as dark as night. The bay at high tide had risen above the level of the clifflike dunes, whipped into powerful waves, threatening the homes directly on the beach.

Quinn said he didn't think it would advance as far as their house, but Molly wasn't so sure. And even without flood damage, the place was taking a beating. If it was dilapidated before, what was it going to be like after this?

The sliding door rattled in its frame, battered by wind-whipped rain and debris. Drafts found every chink, making candle flames shiver and dance. Quinn and Molly didn't speak. They reclined on the cushions, snugly cocooned against the elements, sipping wine and listening to the wailing gales.

The glass had become a mirror, showing the two of them in indolent repose, gilded by candlelight, superimposed on the backdrop of nature's violence. A study in contrasts, Molly thought, staring at her reflection, watching herself lift the juice glass to her lips. She watched Quinn watching her, his gaze on her profile. He tipped the bottle and refilled her glass, and his own.

She supposed she should ask him if he was hungry. It was around dinnertime, but she didn't want to eat, didn't want to move, couldn't bear to break the spell that lulled them like a narcotic.

She couldn't have said how much time passed in this fashion...one hour, two. Their lives outside that one small room ceased to exist. They were castaways on a deserted island, surrounded by an impenetrable blockade of howling wind and rain. Held captive by the forces of darkness. Her mouth quirked at the thought.

Quinn caught her eye in the glass, curious, no doubt, about what had prompted her smile, but unwilling to shatter the trance by asking. Their gazes locked and held for several minutes, and it seemed natural and right, as if nothing else existed that was worthy of their attention.

At last he broke eye contact to set his juice glass aside, and something pumped hard within Molly's body, a burst of anticipation, almost painful. His movements were deceptively unhurried as he took the glass from her hands and placed it next to his.

And then he turned back to her, as she'd known he would, to claim her mouth, his lips wine sweet and urgent. His fingers threaded into her hair and he half covered her. His weight, his heat, the pressure of his body, maddened her.

Their lips clung as if made for this; their limbs twined as if made for this. Her hands clutched at his shoulders, his back, not tenderly but with a bone-deep craving. His tongue stroked her, slid deep to taste her, and she arched into him with a strangled whimper, needing this and so much more.

He caressed the bare skin of her back revealed by her halter top. When his thumb traced the sensitive outside curve of her breast at the edge of the cloth, she wrenched her mouth from his, feeling light-headed, needing air.

Quinn's eyes were even more arresting by candle-light, dangerously intense as he stared down at her. His fingertips lightly stroked up the edge of her halter top, from her waist to her shoulder and around her neck. He tugged on the drawstring tie, and automatically she grabbed his wrist. The wind screamed in her ear, the rain drummed the glass, almost but not quite drowning out the warning voice in her head.

"So shy," he murmured, searching her eyes. "I've seen you before. You weren't shy then."

She tried to bluff, but knew the instant he saw through it, to the yearning she couldn't hope to conceal. He captured her wrists in one hand and reached around her neck to untie the drawstring. Then his fingers slid under her waist to loosen the bow there, leaving the halter top in place but completely unfastened.

He released her wrists. "Take this off."

Molly bit back a spontaneous giggle. Quinn smiled a question.

"Take this off," the sheik commands. *"Dance for me."*

"Maybe I'll tell you about it someday," she said, and pulled the cloth away. The air felt cool on her bare torso, but there was nothing cool in Quinn's gaze.

He lounged on his side next to her, propped on an elbow. His breath drifted over her bare flesh, exciting every nerve ending. His fingers lightly skimmed her belly. They lingered at her navel, just peeking over the top of her sweat shorts, igniting little sparks that made her stomach quiver.

He trailed his fingertips around one breast. Molly felt the nipple pucker. She watched, breathless, as his head slowly lowered and his mouth closed over it. Gasping, she clung to him. Sanity fled under the heat, the suction, the lithe strength of his tongue.

She saw the two of them in the glass, his dark head at her breast, her fingers tangled in his hair. She saw something close to pain on her own face, the wild wanting she'd managed to tame for so long straining at the leash.

He raised his head. She read it in his eyes even before he said, "It's time."

7

QUINN DREW MOLLY to her knees and moved behind her on the quilt. "Look," he said, nodding toward their reflection, pressing a kiss to her shoulder. "I swear I've never seen anything so beautiful."

She looked. And saw herself, bare to the waist, her long hair loose and disheveled—a candlelit ghost image layered on the roaring storm behind the glass. She saw Quinn, too, saw his hands cup her breasts. He lifted them, caressed them. He plucked the tips, gently, stealing her breath.

Molly closed her eyes, shutting out the image of her own helpless need, the flared nostrils, the flush of desire. Quinn whispered in her ear, "Watch with me, Molly. You're so lovely like this."

Stubbornly she kept her eyes shut until she felt him knee her legs apart. One muscular arm was banded around her middle, dark against her paler skin. She could only stare, mesmerized, as the fingers of his other hand slipped under the rolled hem of her shorts, under the elastic edge of her underpants. She flinched when he touched her right there, where she was slick and swollen and more than ready. His arm tightened around her.

"Uh-uh-uh, watch," he chided as her eyelids fluttered, and she did. She watched her body rock into the skillful play of his fingers. He varied his touch, faster, slower, circling the tiny point where all sensation converged.

His finger pushed deep within, and her breath left in a rush. She grabbed his arm like a lifeline. Her soft, panting gasps mirrored the rhythmic pressure of his hand, until the exquisite tension peaked and snapped and her mind splintered with her climax.

Her body pumped hard and Quinn felt it; he told her so. Some wanton part of her responded to the rough, crude words he whispered in her ear, stoking her release until black spots began to crowd her vision.

Limp and sated, she gulped air, even as Quinn yanked her shorts and underpants off in one swift motion. Something shiny flashed out of his pocket, a small square packet. A moment later he was pushing into her from behind, his face stark and savage in the glass.

Molly shouted, awed by the stunning pressure, the glut of pure sensation. His gaze remained riveted on hers as he pressed slowly, inexorably, into her. She greeted each short thrust with a sharp cry of fulfillment until he was fully seated. He felt enormous inside her, an overwhelming presence.

His hands were everywhere, it seemed, urging her toward the pinnacle yet again as he hammered into her hard and fast. As another orgasm rocketed through her, Molly struggled to keep her eyes open, and was rewarded by the sight of Quinn's face as he, too, tumbled over the edge.

They slumped onto all fours, then collapsed onto the quilt. Quinn's heart drummed her back through his T-shirt. It took several minutes for the din of the hurricane to register over the roar of Molly's pulse in her ears.

Quinn seemed to sense the exact moment that his weight ceased being welcome, and rolled off her heavily. She didn't have the strength to open her eyes, but heard discreet movements as he righted himself, the rustle of clothing, the murmur of a zipper. He abandoned her briefly, returning with a soft blanket, in which he lovingly swaddled her.

"It's not fair," she mumbled sleepily, prying her eyes open.

"What's not fair?" His voice was a honeyed rumble in her ear as he tucked the blanket around her shoulders.

"I've never seen you without your clothes. You've seen me, you know, like, totally bare-butt naked. Twice." She tugged on the hem of his shorts. "Take all this off." With a giddy chuckle she added, "Dance for me." She rolled over, stretching languorously, and watched him pull off his T-shirt.

He stood and dropped his shorts. "I'll be happy to dance for you. With or without veils?" He kicked away his briefs and extended his arms to the sides, presenting himself for his lover's inspection.

Molly folded her arms under her head and stared. Quinn really was a magnificently constructed man. And God bless him, he was already hard again. "No veils," she said. "I was thinking more along the lines of the, uh, horizontal hula."

"I don't know, those grass skirts itch like the devil." He slipped beneath the blanket and hauled her to him, giving her her first intoxicating taste of skin-to-skin Quinn. He said, "What say we try this hula thing, like, totally bare-butt naked?"

"NOT EXACTLY WHAT I MEANT when I said make yourself at home."

Alarm bells clanged inside Quinn's unconscious head. Even in slumber, he knew he shouldn't be hearing another man's voice. Not when he and Molly lay sprawled on her bed under a thin sheet, naked and tangled and depleted from a night of nonstop loving. Laboriously he forced himself awake and cracked an eye open.

His muttered curse made Phil Owen smile. It wasn't a pleasant smile.

Quinn glanced at Molly. The sheet covered only her lower body, but at least she was lying on her stomach. Not that Phil didn't know what the flip side looked like, but that was history. Molly was Quinn's now. He pulled the sheet up to her neck and sat up, automatically glancing around for his clothes.

Phil's smile turned meaner. "They're in the living room."

"What the hell are you doing here?"

"Checking out the hurricane damage. No one answered my knock. I don't have to ask what *you're* doing up here." He stared pointedly at Molly, who'd begun to stir.

Her head came up. She looked over her shoulder and frowned in puzzlement. "Phil?" Groggily she sat up, making no concessions to modesty—until she intercepted Quinn's dark scowl, at which point she promptly jerked the sheet up to her shoulders.

Her wary expression told Quinn she hadn't forgotten his obsession with secrecy for the sake of his career. His career had been the furthest thing from his mind last night when he'd been consumed with the need to possess Molly, to pleasure her, to drive himself into her.

Now that discretion was no longer an option, he had trouble recalling exactly why it had seemed so important. It was as if his priorities had suddenly been realigned to fit a new, improved Quinn.

Molly had come into his life and that was all that mattered. Everything else would just have to work itself out somehow.

Quinn got to his feet and faced Phil's corrosive gaze head-on. He felt vulnerable enough stark naked with his ex-boss standing there in his crisp "vacation uniform" of a white polo shirt and knife-pleated slacks; he wasn't going to sit looking up at him, too. He never blinked as a primitive, unspoken, purely male exchange arced between them.

Molly rose, wrapping the sheet around herself. "Phil, did you stop for breakfast on the way up? I'll put on some coffee."

Quinn growled, "He doesn't want any damn coffee."

"Sure I do." Phil's expression was deceptively benign. "Molly knows just how I like it."

"Half-caf," she said, with a yawn. "Just a touch of low-fat milk, right? And most of a packet of Sweet'n Low, only I don't have any, and neither does Quinn. Is sugar okay?"

"Sugar's fine."

Quinn gaped at her. "Why don't you fry him up some bacon and eggs while you're at it? Maybe whip up some pancakes?"

His sarcasm was lost on Mellow Molly. "Sure, if he wants. Maybe you can get started while I cop a shower."

What are you doing? he wanted to shout. *This is the son of a bitch who coerced you! Slandered you! Cheated you!* How could she stand there chatting cordially with Phil as if none of that had happened? Quinn felt like shaking her.

Phil watched Molly walk out of the room, trailing the sheet, which had begun to slip. His gaze lingered a little too long, a little too knowingly, on all the wrong parts. Or all the right parts, depending how you looked at it. Deliberately trying to rattle Quinn's cage, no doubt.

Consider it rattled, you bastard.

Quinn didn't linger. He stalked to the living room and yanked on his shorts as Molly gathered her clothes from the quilt on the floor. He ignored her attempts to make eye contact. His temper was too close to the surface. He didn't even know who he was angry at—or rather, who he was more angry at.

In the past few weeks, Quinn had come to appreciate Molly's sanguine nature, her philosophical outlook. But the time had come to show some grit!

She headed down the hall, passing Phil, who laid his hand on her bare shoulder and murmured something in her ear. The two of them shared a private smile before she disappeared into the bathroom.

The canny devil was wearing a cream-lapping grin when he joined Quinn in the living room. Was that his game, then—to act sweet as pie to the woman he'd publicly vilified, simply to drive a wedge between her and Quinn?

Phil perused the stacked lawn furniture, the taped windows. He gave special attention to the rumpled quilt and sofa cushions on the floor. When he turned back to Quinn, his smile had been replaced by a sneer of pure venom. He asked how long Quinn had been making love with Molly, couching the question in the crudest language.

Quinn had no intention of answering that. Molly was right; she'd been right all along. Phil no longer had a claim on her, which meant there was no need for secrecy. But by the same token, whatever happened between Quinn and Molly was none of his damn business.

When his question was greeted with silence, Phil said, "Call me naive, but I never figured you'd go sniffing around my ex. I mean, the woman's poison. This isn't news to you. If you wanted to get your rocks off, why didn't you snag one of the beach babes? Or a town girl. Easy pickings."

"Don't know what possessed her to walk away from a prince like you. I'm curious about something. How long before the wedding were you sitting on that prenup? Just waiting to spring it on her at the last minute?"

"It's called hedging your bets." Phil shook his head sadly. "I used to think you were savvy, Quinn. A real up-and-comer. Course, if you were so damn savvy, you wouldn't have messed around with *my ex!*" he suddenly hollered, tapping his chest. He flushed brick red; a muscle jumped in his cheek. He spread his palms. "You see what I'm saying here? That doesn't strike you as a monumentally self-destructive act?"

Now that the worst had happened, Quinn could only marvel at his previous tunnel vision. He almost laughed. What were the threats of this spiteful, manipulative man compared to what he'd found in Molly's arms?

Phil added, "Know what I'm going to do soon as I get back to New York? I'm gonna make a few phone calls, have a chat with every major agency. You better learn how to make Happy Meals, buddy boy."

"I'm not worried," Quinn answered easily. "I don't think you have that kind of juice in the business. I did, but now I'm not so sure."

Phil took a step closer, quivering with rage. "You don't think I could destroy you?" He snapped his fingers. "Like that?"

"I'll risk it." He'd risk that and more for Molly.

"Get the hell out of my house. Now."

Quinn had anticipated this. Molly was still in the shower; he heard it running. He grabbed his shirt and briefs, shoved his feet in his deck shoes and headed downstairs without a word. By the time Phil appeared on the threshold, Quinn had already thrown all his clothes and toiletries into his luggage. He swiftly made his way through the rooms, tossing his personal possessions into the plastic milk crate he'd brought with him. He left the food behind. Phil watched silently, arms folded over his chest.

A minute later Quinn slammed the trunk of his car and started back into the house. To Molly. She'd want to leave with him, he was sure.

Phil blocked the entrance. He held out his hand. "Keys."

"Molly!" Quinn called. Was she still in the shower?

"If you're not off my property in ten seconds, I'm calling the cops. Give me the damn keys!"

Quinn worked the two beach-house keys off his key ring and hurled them over the roof of Phil's silver BMW, into the patch of poison ivy that passed for a side yard. Phil cursed ripely.

Molly pounded down the stairs, wet hair flying, zipping her short denim skirt. "Quinn!" she cried, pushing past Phil. "What's going on?"

"What's going on is that I've been asked to vacate the premises. I'm leaving, Molly."

She turned to Phil, with a perplexed frown. "Because of me? I didn't think you still cared about me that way."

Phil touched her cheek. "Neither did I, till I saw you with someone else."

"I don't believe this," Quinn muttered.

Phil's performance had nothing to do with tender feelings for Molly, and everything to do with male territorial rights. He didn't want her, but his ego couldn't bear to see her happy with Quinn. Her failure to see Phil's chest-thumping for what it was frustrated and angered Quinn.

"Are you satisfied, Molly?" he snapped. "You see now why I wanted to be discreet? You'll be happy to know he's planning to blacklist me in the industry. Don't say I didn't call this one."

She blinked, clearly stung. Phil put his arm around her shoulders and she didn't shake it off. That was the coup de grâce, watching the smug bastard touch her, as if he had a right. *And she let him!*

"I don't think you have to worry about your career, Quinn," she said. "There's something I haven't—"

"If I listened to you, I wouldn't worry about a damn thing, would I!" He gesticulated angrily. "My life would just roll along with no direction, and to hell with my goals, my dreams, everything I've busted my butt for!"

"Quinn, let me tell—"

"Save it. I do have to worry about my career now, Molly, and none of your useless feel-good platitudes are going to pull it out of the fire."

Molly didn't move a muscle; she just stood staring at him. Finally she said, "You're upset, Quinn. That's why you're lashing out at me. I can understand that."

"You know what?" He rounded the Mercedes. "I don't want your understanding. You're *too* damn understanding."

Phil said, "I don't think your 'understanding' was what he was after, Molly."

She never took her eyes from Quinn as he slid behind the wheel and started the car. He'd thought his imminent departure would goad her into action, but she said nothing, did nothing. He wouldn't humiliate himself by asking her to leave with him. If she wanted to, she'd have said so. One thing about Molly, she didn't play coy.

Would she take Phil back now? Or more to the point, would she let him manipulate her into believing he wanted her back? Would she let him use her again, savage her feelings again? Probably. Molly and her ex looked pretty damn cozy from where Quinn sat.

He executed a two-point turn to nose onto the road, then stuck his head out the window. "Hey, Phil. Give my best to Ben, will ya?"

Phil's eye twitched. "Ben who?"

"'Ben who?' Ben Curran, you big kidder. Your cousin. First cousin on your mother's side, am I right? The guy who replaced me. Inexperienced and more than a little incompetent, from what I hear." And then, as if he hadn't put a fine enough point on it, he added, "He's the reason you fired me. You remember Ben."

Phil looked like he didn't want to.

Molly appeared more resigned than distraught. If she'd shed one tear, if she'd silently pleaded with that expressive face of hers—if she'd looked like she gave a damn!—he might have stayed and fought for her. He might have insisted she get in the car and leave with him. But she didn't.

Quinn gunned the accelerator and reached for his road map.

8

MOLLY WATCHED the butter yellow Mercedes disappear around a curve in the road.

He'll be back. He just needs some time alone. He'll come back to me.

She realized all her concentration had been centered on Quinn when she suddenly noticed things she hadn't before. Such as a pressure on her shoulder that turned out to be Phil's arm.

She promptly stepped away from him. "Did you really threaten to blacklist Quinn?"

"It was no threat, Molly. First thing tomorrow morning, I'm working the phone."

She sighed. "Well, you have to do what you have to do, I guess. It's your way to respond with aggression, and I understand that."

"I admire your understanding nature, Molly. I really do. That's the difference between me and Quinn."

"Oh, there are *so many* differences between you and Quinn! I didn't realize that before, but now I do."

"Well, better late than never. Although I suppose I shouldn't be surprised that you were attracted to someone who reminded you of me. After everything we shared." He edged closer, and she smoothly sidled away from him.

"You know, speaking of working the phone," she said, "I've been kind of burning up the long-distance wires myself lately. Don't worry, I used my credit card. They won't show up on your bill."

"Oh, that wasn't necessary." Phil smiled magnanimously.

"Well, I don't want to take advantage, you know?"

As he started to reach for her, Molly turned and gingerly made her way barefoot through the poison-ivy-studded minefield of a yard to the ancient rusted swing set. She perched on a cracked plastic swing and began to lazily rock herself.

The sun caught something bright on the ground. "Are those your keys?" she asked.

"Uh, yes. If you wouldn't mind tossing them to me."

"They're, like, right in a patch of poison ivy. I do mind."

"Then just leave the damn things."

She pitied the families with young children who reserved this house for their vacation, only to discover that the decks were dangerously rotted, the swing set was falling apart and you couldn't toss a Frisbee around without risking a bout of poison ivy. She'd spoken to Phil about it so many times. He'd always yessed her to death with false promises of fixing the place up. Talk about penny wise, pound foolish!

He stood some distance away in the dirt at the edge of the yard, eyeing it as if it were a moat stocked with giant squid. "So. Mind if I ask who you've been chatting with long distance?"

"Anyone who might be hiring a copy editor."

"Ah. Any nibbles?"

"As a matter of fact, yes," she said. "You know Randall Harkin?"

"Randy Harkin. Sure. Editor in chief of *Advertising Today*."

She beamed. "Gosh, you know just about everyone in the industry, don't you?"

He puffed up. "I didn't get where I am by burying my head in the sand."

"You can say that again! Randy thinks your whole professional career is, like, *so* fascinating."

"He does? You two talked about me?"

"Did we talk about you!" She chuckled. "We hardly talked about anything else!"

Phil's eyes lit with excitement. "I haven't been profiled in *Ad Today* in years. Maybe I'll give Randy a call—"

"Save your quarter. It's a done deal. And I'm not talking any measly one-column profile either, but a *whole dang feature article!* I convinced him you were newsworthy." She buffed her nails on her T-shirt. "What do you think of *them* apples?"

Phil stared at her in slack-jawed gratitude, and even took a step toward her before leaping back out of the moat. "You did that? For me?"

She gave him her most angelic smile. "Hey. It's the least I could do after all you've done for *me*."

"So who's writing the article?"

She preened. "You're looking at her."

"*You?*"

"He hired me!"

"What?" he said. "Over the phone?"

"No no. We met. Turned out he was coming up to Nantucket the weekend before last, so I asked if I could hook up with him there. Quinn drove me to

Hyannis Port and I took the ferry across. Randy is *such* a nice guy, Phil. Did you know he's some kind of champion deep-sea fisherman? We took his yacht out and he caught this *humongous*—"

"Wait. Back up. *You're* writing the article about me?"

"It's already written. Randy hired me as associate editor, but I'm free to pitch articles, too. Oh, and guess what I found out when I called around. Just about *everyone* pays way more than you do! How about that! They could learn a thing or two from you about trimming costs, huh?"

His mouth worked soundlessly for a few moments.

"Don't you want to know what's in the article?" she asked. "Come on, I know you're dying to ask me."

"Well. Uh, I imagine it chronicles my long history in the business, my award-winning—"

Molly waved away such prosaic details. "That's the *public* Phil Owen, the Phil Owen everyone already knows. I thought the readers would be interested in the *real* you. The man behind the marble desk and the thousand-dollar suits. An insider's perspective. You know."

Phil stared at her for long moments. His eyes widened. "What have you done?"

"The last-minute, one-sided prenuptial agreement. The blatant nepotism. Some of your more, shall we say, innovative business practices. They're all in there. Plus a whole bunch of revealing quotes. I did phone interviews with a lot of people you've dealt with over the years and they were all real enthusiastic about sharing anecdotes. And best of all?

Check it out—you've got the cover! Randy, like, *flipped* over this article!''

Phil's eyes bulged; his color spiked alarmingly. Molly was thankful for the poison ivy separating them.

He muttered, "*He* put you up to this.''

"Who, Quinn? Nope. He knows about the job, but not the article. I have my own reasons for keeping it to myself. Though I did get my inspiration from a comment he once made, about an open letter.''

Phil pulled himself up. Pointed his finger at her. "You are going to kill that article, Molly.''

"Okay.''

He blinked. "What?''

"There's still time to pull it. If you're sure that's what you want.''

He sagged in relief—for about a second before his eyes got that squinty, suspicious look. "All right, how much?''

She slapped her thigh. "Now, see, I'm not surprised you assume this is about money. You've always had your eye on the bottom line. I ask you, is it any wonder you're at the top of the food chain?''

"Cut the crap, Molly. What do I have to do to kill that tell-all piece?''

"It's not what you have to *do*. It's what you have to *not* do. Namely, *not* sabotage Quinn's career. Which I know deep in your heart you really don't want to do.''

She saw him thinking about it, saw him looking at her as though she'd evolved from her original spineless state into some kind of unfamiliar vertebrate lifeform in the space of one short month.

What can I tell you? I've never been in love before.

Phil crossed his arms. "There's no article. No job at *Ad Today*. You're bluffing."

Laughter burst from her. "Bluffing? Me? I can't bluff! Just ask your brother."

Phil took a deep breath. "Very well. I won't make those phone calls. I won't interfere with Quinn's career in any way. You have my word."

"And that means so much to me, your giving your word like that. But you know, sometimes people forget what they gave their word on, and I know you've been the victim of that kind of memory loss in the past, so I'm going to keep that article on file. And update it on a regular basis. Just in case."

In truth, Molly had no desire to destroy Phil's reputation. She'd assumed—hoped—the piece would remain unpublished even as she'd pitched it to Randy. Its sole function was as an insurance policy in the event Phil did indeed threaten Quinn's career. It had served its purpose.

"You know, now that I think of it," she said, "there is something you have to do."

One eyebrow rose questioningly.

"Fix this place up," she said. "I mean *really* fix it up. Inside and out. And hire a weekly gardening service to make sure anything growing around here is safe to walk on and play in. Just think. You get this place shipshape, you can charge much more than your usual six seventy-five per apartment per week."

"How'd you know—" He cut himself off.

"I put in a call to the local realtor you use. Sylvie was so *surprised* to learn how much you'd charged me. She wants to have a little chat with you, I think. Nice lady, Sylvie. Did you know her aunt Thea was Elvis's manicurist?"

"I assume that's the next item of extortion." Phil sounded drained. "A refund of your rent."

"Gosh, thanks! It honestly hadn't occurred to me, but since you're offering, why not?" She wagged her finger at him. "Admit it. You feel better already, knowing you're making things right."

"No."

Was it bluster, or was he really that cold? "I hope you do someday, Phil. I believe there's more to you than you let people see. More...I don't know, more humanity."

He looked at her with something akin to awe. "You really do believe that, don't you? After everything."

"I've had a few glimpses of the real you over the years." She smiled sadly. "You can't convince me it was *all* an act."

He shook his head in wonder, and she saw a little of that humanity peeking through. "I really screwed things up with that prenup, didn't I?"

"It's just as well. It wasn't meant to be."

"No. I suppose not." He studied the yard around the swing set. "I'll get a lawn service out here ASAP. As for the rest of it..." He looked at the dilapidated house. "I'll start calling around. I'm going to Kenya on safari next week—I'll try to get all the repair work lined up before I go."

Phil didn't glance her way again as he strode toward his BMW. "You've read the lease. I'll expect you out of here by noon on the thirty-first."

9

MOLLY FINGERED the tiny scrimshaw charm hanging on a short gold chain just below the hollow of her throat. She imagined she could feel the delicate image etched into the surface. "Thank you for showing me the swan," Quinn had said that night out on her deck.

Thank you for showing me what it feels like to be in love, she thought. Even if it couldn't last. Even if he didn't return her love.

It was July 31, nearly 1:00 a.m. Molly had packed what she could; last-minute items such as her bedding and toiletries would have to wait. She had to be out of the house by noon. Her friend Claire, whose boyfriend lived in Boston, had given Molly a lift to the Cape on one of her trips to visit him. Claire was due to swing by and pick her up in the morning for the trip back to New York.

Restless, Molly grabbed a plaid wool stadium blanket from a half-packed carton and trudged down the stairs. Outside, the night air was cool and heavy with mist. Clouds obscured Cygnus and the other constellations. She slung the small blanket over her shoulders and strolled barefoot the short distance to the beach.

The rough road surface soon gave way to the cool caress of sand. She was going to miss this place. For the rest of her life, she'd never be able to think of it without wondering where Quinn was, what he was doing, who he was with, whether he was happy. She wished that for him and more: happiness and love and, yes, the attainment of each and every one of those momentous fiscal goals he held so dear.

Molly veered to the right, onto the stretch of beach bordered by the field of tall grasses, alive with the trilling of crickets. She steered clear of the handful of beach houses to the left, instinctively shunning human contact. The tide was in and water lapped gently at the shore.

Something sharp scraped her toe and she bent down to retrieve a small scallop shell. She peered at the tiny object by the meager light of the waning crescent moon struggling through cloud cover. She rubbed her fingers over the ridges on both sides, the nick at the bottom. Then she hauled back and chucked it into the bay.

Quinn hadn't come back to her. After three days, Molly was forced to admit she'd called this one wrong. She'd thought all he'd needed was breathing space, a little time to cool off. She'd been so certain he'd felt what she had: the sharp, sweet thrill of discovery; the simple rightness of being with each other.

Should she have left with him? Three days ago she'd known in her heart the answer was no; he needed time alone. It was only when he didn't return, or even call, that doubts began to creep in. Perhaps she should have forced the issue, after all— planted herself in his car and made him take her with him whether he wanted to or not.

No. She was through barging into his life. If he'd wanted her, he'd have let her know by now.

She could have told Quinn about the *Ad Today* article two weeks ago, when she'd first started working on it, but she'd feared that would only muddy the waters, at a time when they were trying to come to grips with their feelings for each other. Although she'd begun to realize that Quinn and Phil were different in every way that mattered, Quinn's continued insistence on secrecy had told her his career still took center stage. It came before everything else, including her.

Molly had needed to know that if and when they made love, it would be because Quinn had opened his heart to her unreservedly, come what may, not because he was relying on the trump card of her tell-all article to keep Phil Owen from wreaking havoc.

And indeed, on that wonderful night when Quinn had shared himself with her, with no mention of Phil or his career or keeping anything under wraps, Molly had felt whole for the first time. Cherished.

When he'd thrown it back in her face the next morning, she'd given him the benefit of the doubt; she'd assumed he hadn't meant his bitter words, that he was just worried for his career.

It had been three days. He'd meant them.

He truly did resent her for bringing Phil's wrath down on his head, as unfair as that was. She'd tried to tell him about the article then, so he'd know he had nothing to fear from Phil, but he'd been too angry to listen.

Molly stopped walking and pulled the blanket more securely around herself. She stood listening to the crickets, and the breeze sighing through the tall grass beyond the berm of sand. From here no houses were visible, no lights. The late hour and damp chill meant the beach was all hers, for which she was grateful. She doubted she could summon up her usual gregariousness tonight.

She looked back the way she'd come and was surprised to see she'd counted her blessings too soon. A lone figure emerged from the gloom, a dark silhouette. Someone trying to decide whether this was a good night for a stroll on the beach, she supposed. *It isn't*, she wanted to yell. *Go away. I was here first.* She sensed him returning her stare, picking up on her inhospitable thoughts, she hoped.

He began to move, not away but toward her. Irritation flared for an instant, until she recognized the fluid, long-legged stride. Even in the dark, at a distance, Molly knew Quinn's walk.

Her emotions rioted. Quinn's presence could mean everything or nothing. He'd returned for some forgotten item, she told herself. It had nothing to do with her.

She watched him approach, hands stuffed in his jeans pockets. The skimpy moonlight gave no clue to his expression until he was standing right in front of her, close enough to touch.

What she saw then made her breath snag. She felt his intimate gaze like a caress, on her hair, her mouth, her eyes. He lifted his hand, slowly, and brushed a fingertip across her eyelashes. "Tears?" he said, his voice heartbreakingly gentle. "Ah, Molly..."

She drew in a shaky breath. "You came back. I—I didn't think..."

He smiled with his eyes, those seductive gigolo eyes that she could stare into forever. "No, I didn't think. Or I thought too much, I don't know. I let my ego get in the way. Maybe Phil and I *are* alike."

"No. You're nothing like him, Quinn. I should've seen it right away, but I was, I don't know, wary."

"Who could blame you?"

Speaking of blame… "You're not still angry with me? For Phil finding out and all that?"

"Molly." He framed her face in his hands. "I never thought that was your fault. Those things I said. I didn't mean them. I was…I didn't mean them. I should've tossed you in the car and made you leave with me. My gut told me not to, but I wish I had."

A watery chuckle escaped her. "We both made the mistake of listening to our instincts."

"I'm an idiot," he said.

"Say it louder. I want everyone to know."

He threw back his head and yelled, "I'm an idiot! Quinn Marshall is an—"

Molly clapped her hand over his mouth. He kissed her palm and twined his fingers through hers.

"I used to think getting on the wrong side of Phil was the worst thing that could happen," Quinn said. "Then it happened and I realized that as long as I had you, nothing else mattered."

Molly bit her lip against a sob of joy and relief. Quinn draped his forearms over her shoulders and tipped his forehead down to hers. They stood that way for several minutes, drinking in each other's nearness and warmth. Finally Molly had to ask.

"Why did you leave? I mean, I know you had to leave because Phil kicked you out, but why did you stay away?"

He kissed her forehead. "I thought you were going to take Phil back."

She could only gape at him, speechless.

"I told you, I'm an idiot. Then I started making

calls, lining up job interviews, and a very interesting story began to emerge. It seems my Mellow Molly has been quite enterprising."

"'Mellow Molly'?" She rolled it around in her mind, then nodded in approval. "Go on."

"Many of the industry people I talked to had been contacted by a charming and delightful young woman working on an article about Phil Owen for *Advertising Today*. And get this, the reporter freely admits she was once *engaged* to the guy, and somehow she gets all these people to share every smarmy detail of their dealings with him. I knew I couldn't be the only one to see that blowhard for what he is, and I was right."

"You reap what you sow."

"Word is, the article was killed. Then it turns out Phil never followed through on his threats to ruin me. You see how an interesting scenario begins to take shape here—one even an idiot like me can't fail to recognize."

"What might that scenario be?"

"Mellow Molly has learned the gentle art of extortion."

She shrugged. "He threatened the man I love."

Quinn sought her eyes in the dark. He took a deep breath. "You beat me to it. I wanted to say it first."

She smiled. "I didn't, like, actually say it, though, did I?"

"No, come to think of it." He brought his lips to her ear and nuzzled aside her hair. His breath was hot, but it was his words that warmed her to her core. "I love you, Molly." He kissed her ear, her temple. "I love you so much it scares me."

"I love you, too," she whispered. "Doesn't scare me at all."

She felt his answering grin. He cupped her face and brought his lips to hers, and the feel of him, the taste of him, made her stupid and clumsy. She slid her arms around him and the blanket started to slip. She made a grab for it, but he caught it first and snugged it around her.

"Is there room under this thing for two?" he asked.

In answer she draped the blanket over his shoulders, and was instantly rewarded. His arm snaked around her back to pull her against him, while the fingers of his other hand pushed through her hair and tipped her head back for a kiss so deep, so possessive, it was just as well he was holding her up.

"Three days," he growled, pressing hard, fast kisses to her face, her throat, stealing her wits. "I don't ever want to be away from you for that long again."

Molly didn't notice he'd managed to unbutton her denim shirt until she felt cool air on her breasts, followed by Quinn's toasty hands. She groaned in helpless pleasure. The zipper of her jeans was next, while she struggled to yank his sweatshirt up and off him. They tottered, off balance, as jeans, underwear and Quinn's shoes were kicked away.

Then he was there, pressed full-length to her, hot and hard and wonderfully impatient, the silky steel of his erection twitching against her belly. She savored the spiraling tension in her own body, a thumping drumbeat of need growing louder and louder, drowning out everything else, everything that wasn't Quinn.

The night sky spun as he lowered her to the

ground, the sand coarse and bumpy under the blanket. She never had a chance to catch her breath, with his hands here and his mouth there and her body arching and opening and she was ready so ready and she needed him *now*.

She told him so, panting, pleading, with no shame at all because this was Quinn and her deep need began and ended with this man.

He kissed her mouth. "Trust me," he whispered, and kissed a path down her body.

She whimpered and clutched him even as his hands came under her knees to open her wider, even as his hot breath and hotter mouth wrenched a startled cry of pleasure from her. He parted her with his fingers, tasted and teased her with eager delight. He did things with his supple lips and long, strong tongue and gently scraping teeth that she'd never even imagined. Dimly, through the haze of her gathering climax, she recalled Quinn describing himself as "inventive."

He raised his head. "I sure as heck am *what*?"

"I wasn't talking to you." She pushed his head down. "Don't stop!"

Molly felt him chuckle as he pressed one last deep, intimate kiss to her drenched flesh. He moved with stunning speed and suddenly was inside her, deep, deeper, and she could only thank heaven Quinn loved her because the wild, guttural sounds she was making might have scared off a less devoted man.

One of his hands cupped the back of her neck while the other slid under her bottom to lift her. Her body coiled tighter with each long, powerful thrust, and suddenly her orgasm was within reach, hovering like some great bird—a swan, she thought—

awaiting only the merest signal to alight and carry her off.

She smiled, and Quinn smiled, understanding, and he abandoned all restraint. She welcomed his rough, hammering strokes, met them, matched them. The swan touched down and she took wing with it, soaring out of herself even as an explosion of sensation rocked the deepest core of her.

Afterward, they lay in a torpid heap, their hearts galloping in tandem. Molly sighed, a deep, cleansing exhalation. She stroked Quinn's back and kissed his closed eyelids. He emitted a satisfied little grunt and offered a blind kiss that landed on the side of her nose.

Something wet plopped in her eye and she blinked. She felt a drop on her arm, and one on her foot. "Quinn, it's raining."

He responded with an incoherent mumble. She tried to lever herself up, but the deadweight on top of her wasn't budging. She pushed at him, chuckling. "Quinn! It's starting to rain. Get up."

His eyes drifted open and he smiled lazily, and she wondered if anything had ever looked as sinfully provocative as this man's smile. Even when those first few drops turned into a steady light rainfall, he resisted her attempts to rise.

"You should be more laid-back, like me," he drawled, pinning her arms as she laughed helplessly, squeezing her eyes shut against the rain.

Abruptly he came up on one elbow. "Oh, no."

"What?"

"We didn't use anything."

"Oh. Wow. I didn't even think about it...."

"Me, neither. That's never happened to me before,

Molly—that I got so carried away I forgot protection."

"Well, at least it's not my fertile time."

He kissed her and got up, gathering their clothes. "There's no time that's a hundred percent safe. I'm sorry." He pulled on his underwear and chinos, his expression thoughtful. "I wouldn't be, though. If you got pregnant. Sorry, I mean." He sighed. "I'm not saying this very well."

Molly went to him, half-dressed, heedless of the cold rain. She held his face in both hands and made him look at her. "You're saying it just fine, Quinn." She brushed her thumb over his lips and he kissed it. "I love you and you love me. How could a child of ours be anything but a blessing?"

He stroked her bare upper arms. "I didn't mean to lay this on you so soon. Didn't want to scare you off." He took a deep breath. His hands tightened on her arms. "I want to marry you, Molly."

Her heart swelled, stinging her eyes, stealing her voice.

He said, "I know you were burned once. I won't rush you." He smiled, and touched her belly tenderly. "As long as there's no reason to. But those are my intentions. You have a right to know."

She opened her mouth to speak.

"And before you ask," he said, "I'm not signing any prenup, so don't even think about it."

"What, I'm supposed to trust you with my vast holdings?"

"I've discovered I'm kind of old-fashioned when it comes to marriage. For better or for worse, we're in it together. Besides, a prenup might backfire on me...."

He gave her a wry grin. "After all, you're the one who's gainfully employed."

"No job yet?"

"I've only been at it a few days. I've gotten a couple of good leads, but nothing solid." He pulled his sweatshirt down over his rain-soaked head. "What a pompous jerk I was, preaching at you about your money situation, and here you manage to nail this fabulous position without setting foot off the Cape!"

"I recall a ferry ride to Nantucket."

"Are you always so literal?"

She snarled in frustration, trying to push her arms into her rain-soaked shirtsleeves.

"Don't bother," Quinn said, commandeering the shirt and enveloping her in the damp, gritty blanket. "It wouldn't stay on for long, anyway." He slid his feet into the deck shoes and wrapped an arm around her back.

They retraced their way down the rain-washed beach and trudged up the sandy incline to the parking lot. The house came into view, the windows of the top floor glowing in welcome. On impulse Molly made a dash for it, leaving Quinn holding the blanket.

Naked from the waist up, she sprinted through the parking lot and straight down the middle of the road, laughing at Quinn's outraged bellow as he raced to overtake her with the blanket. As if anyone was likely to see her bare bosom in the rain-drenched middle of the night!

She stopped and did a little victory dance right there in the center of the road, twirling in the rain, whooping with glee. Quinn didn't bother with the blanket, he simply slung her over his shoulder and marched across the yard, gravely enumerating those parts of her that were for his eyes only, now that they were engaged.

"We are?" she asked the small of his back, not quite ready to agree and put him out of his misery, eagerly anticipating days or even weeks of Quinn's inventive brand of persuasion.

He kicked open the front door and stalked up the stairs. "*Practically* engaged, then. Close enough."

Mellow Molly decided she was going to enjoy spending the rest of her life scandalizing the man with the gigolo eyes.

August

by
Patricia Ryan

1

SALLY CURRAN OPENED her eyes and sat up in bed.

Huh? The alarm clock was mute; it was almost seven a.m.

Wood creaked. She cocked her head to listen.

Another creak.

Footsteps?

Nah. It was just her latent fear coming to the surface. Ever since she got here yesterday, she'd been fretting about spending a month in this big house all alone, and now her paranoia had made her start imagining—

Creak.

She turned toward the window that looked out on the ground-floor wraparound deck. Something dark shadowed the curtain and moved on. *Creak. Creak.*

Omigod. Sally vaulted out of bed, feeling chilled to the bone despite the sweltering heat. *Omigod, omigod.*

Creak. Creak. The footsteps, slow and weighty, were heading away from the bedroom wing and toward the living area—where the only phone was.

Be calm, be calm, be calm. Sally pushed her hair out of her eyes, licked her dry lips. She felt vulnerable in her sleeveless white cotton nightgown, but taking the time to get dressed was out of the question. She walked through the bedroom door and down the hallway on gelatinous legs.

On the threshold of the living room, she paused and listened; the footsteps had been heading in this direction.

Nothing.

The phone sat beside a battered old record player on the sideboard next to one of the two sliding glass doors, the one facing the side yard with its dilapidated swing set, and the grassy field between the house and the beach beyond. Sally stepped into the living room, weighing her options—dial 911 or go outside and run.

A movement to the right drew her gaze to the dining area. A dark-haired man stood outside the other sliding glass door, big as life—bigger—and...*omigod*. Half-naked. He didn't notice her, his attention consumed by a little metal bar he was jiggling, at the edge of the door, near the lock.

The door popped open with a rusty screech. He shoved it open the rest of the way, slipped the little bar into the back pocket of his cutoffs—the only thing he had on other than a pair of work boots—and looked at her.

Nothing separated them now except a dining table and about twenty feet of sandy floor tiles. Sally turned and sprinted toward the front door.

Scream, you idiot! She tried, but all that would come out of her throat was a pathetic little whine of panic. *Scream, scream,* she commanded herself as her fingers fumbled with the unfamiliar door lock.

"Hey, listen..."

She looked back over her shoulder to see the intruder striding toward her, his long legs eating up the distance between them way too fast.

A shriek of unbridled terror tore from her lungs. *Finally!*

"Whoa." That stopped the guy in his tracks. "Hey, listen, don't scream."

The lock gave way. She whipped the door open, leaped off the front stoop and raced through the front yard of sand and weeds toward the road.

The ground thudded. He was right behind her.

She screamed again, or tried to. She opened her mouth, but her howl was silenced almost instantly by a giant hand whipping around from behind. *No!*

An arm encircled her waist. Legs tangled with hers. As the sand rose up to meet her, her assailant twisted around so that it was he who hit the ground, with her on top.

"Listen to me...."

She tried to get up, but he held her tight. She drew in a breath to scream, but again he slammed his hand over her mouth, rolling over so that she was trapped beneath him.

"You're gonna wake up the neighbors."

That's the idea. She squirmed and struggled, but it was hopeless. He must have carried over two hundred and twenty pounds of hard-packed muscle on his jumbo, economy-size frame. He held her arms pinioned, and although she writhed frantically, her long nightgown prevented her from moving her legs enough to kick him.

"Look," he said, his gaze boring into hers. "I'm not gonna hurt you."

She bit his hand, hard. He yowled. *All right if I hurt you?*

She sucked in another lungful of air.

"My name's Tom O'Hearn," he said in a rush.

"I'm your upstairs neighbor, I just got here from Boston, I drove half the night, I didn't mean to scare you, for God's sake don't scream again."

He looked at her imploringly with glow-in-the-dark blue eyes. She felt someone's heart thundering, but it was impossible to say whose it was, with them fused together like a couple of sweaty teenagers.

"I don't know anything about any upstairs neighbor," she managed to gasp.

"You're Sally Curran, right? Phil Owen's cousin?"
She nodded.

"He didn't tell you I was coming?"
Sally shook her head. She'd rented the bottom half of the ramshackle beach house from Phil for the month of August. Phil hadn't said anything about another tenant, and she'd just assumed she had the whole place to herself.

"I'd tell you to call him so he can confirm that I'm supposed to be here, but I don't think there are any phones in the African bush. Isn't he in Kenya playing the great white hunter for the next few weeks?"

Sally nodded.

"So how can I prove to you that I'm harmless?" the intruder asked in his deep, slightly rough-edged voice.

Harmless? Tom O'Hearn had arms and legs like tree trunks. His chest was a wall of brawn, damp and softly furred; the hair there tickled her with every ragged breath she took. "You can start by getting off me."

He looked down, stared unblinkingly for a moment, then took hold of the neckline of her nightgown.

"Hey, what are you—"

"Sorry." He pulled the thin cotton across her chest to cover her up. "I guess some buttons came undone.... You were sort of..."

"Omigod." She'd been lying there with her gown gaping open, exposed, or half-exposed, to this total stranger. Not that there was that much to see. Sally was and had always been the Amazing Breastless Wonder. But still. She clutched the gown to keep it closed. "Get off me."

As he eased his weight off her, she noticed something that somewhat reassured her. His ears had turned pink. How dangerous could he be if he blushed at the sight of a bare breast?

She rebuttoned her nightgown as he stood and dusted himself off. No need to give him any more of a show than she already had. He offered her his hand, and after a moment's hesitation she took it and let him help her to her feet.

He appraised her discreetly as she rose, taking in her long-limbed bod. When they stood facing each other, she realized he was only a couple of inches taller than she, which would put him at six-two or thereabouts. He'd looked bigger while he was jimmying open that glass door.

Oh, yeah... "What did you think you were doing, breaking into my half of the house?"

"I didn't think you were here yet." He indicated the scrubby property with a sweep of his arm. "I didn't see your car."

"It started gasping and wheezing while I was driving up Route 6 yesterday. I took it to the shop in town and rode my bike back."

He grinned. "You bike? Me, too." He nodded toward something behind her.

She turned and saw a black pickup truck that had escaped her notice during her mad flight from the house. TOM O'HEARN was painted in white on the door, and below that, S•P•O•O•S•E. *Spoose*? A racing bike, also black, was strapped to the back of the truck.

"Look," he said, rasping a hand over his stubbly jaw, "I really am sorry for scaring you like that. I can imagine what you thought."

"That's all right," she said, swatting sand off her legs. Her heart still hadn't stopped hammering.

Tom stuck his hands in his pockets, stretching the worn denim across his hips—the only lean part of him. He had the kind of linebacker build that seemed to take up way more space than it really did. His skin had tanned the color of toast, which was probably why his eyes looked so radiant. "Phil really should have told you I was coming."

"Can't argue with you there." She dragged a still-shaky hand through her hair. "But it's just like Phil to neglect to mention something like that. He tends to be kind of…"

"Self-involved?"

"Preoccupied."

He smiled crookedly. "I made a pot of coffee. It should be done by now. You want some?"

"Coffee?"

"It's these little beans they grow in Colombia. They roast them and grind them up—"

"I'd like some coffee," she said with a grudging smile. "Just give me a minute to get dressed."

"I'll bring it out to the table on the downstairs deck."

Back in her room, Sally changed into shorts and a

Road Runner T-shirt, washed her face and ran a comb through her hair. As an afterthought, she brushed her teeth. Usually she didn't brush until after she'd had breakfast, but there was no point in exposing this guy to her morning mouth. Not that he'd get close enough so it would matter. Heck, she'd already been as close to him as she was ever likely to get, so the damage was done.

On her way out of the bathroom, she doubled back, yanked open the cabinet under the sink, which creaked on its one good hinge, and retrieved her little makeup kit. A hint of mascara just to counteract the morning puffiness around her eyes. She pinched her cheeks and groaned with self-disgust. *Who are you? Scarlett O'Hara? Get a grip.*

She found him on the back deck tucking into a white bakery box filled with doughnuts. He'd put on a well-aged gray T-shirt with a little hole in one of the shoulder seams. The implication, considering the Schwarzeneggeresque breadth of his shoulders, was that the shirt had been subjected to more strain than it could bear.

He gazed at her chest with a smile of appreciation. "I'm crazy about the Road Runner."

"Me, too." She sat across from him, telling herself to relax. This wasn't a date, for crying out loud. This guy lived here. They both lived here. They were going to live here together. For the rest of the summer.

"How do you like it?"

She blinked at him.

"Your coffee." He lifted a glass carafe off the pot holder it was sitting on. "How do you like it?"

"Black, no sugar."

"Yeah?" He grinned. "Me, too."

He poured her coffee into a thick, chipped mug with blue stripes around the edges. They were the mugs that came with the house. She'd found a set of them in her own cabinet yesterday. It was the mug she was looking at, not his hand, but she couldn't help noticing as her gaze zeroed in on the ring finger—the mug happened to be in his left hand—that there was no wedding ring there. No telltale tan line, either.

She raised the cup to her mouth and blew on it. His gaze strayed to her mouth.

"So, are you married?" he asked.

She choked on her first, tentative sip of coffee.

"You all right?" He got up and circled the table, sitting on the bench next to her.

She nodded, coughing and sputtering as heat flooded her face. *Nice goin', Curran. Can you think of any more ways to embarrass yourself?*

"Put your arms up." Tom grasped her hands and raised them over her head, holding them there while he patted her between the shoulder blades.

"I'm fine," she croaked. "Really." His fingers felt as rough as a cat's tongue on her sensitive inner wrists.

He lowered her arms. The hand that had been patting her began moving in languid circles on her back; she felt his calluses even through her T-shirt.

"You've got one bony back," he said.

"I'm bony all over, in case you hadn't noticed."

"I don't know about that." His hand stilled on her lower back. "You've got kind of a Julia Roberts thing going there, except for the blond hair. Are you a model?"

"I did a little runway work in college. I teach English now."

"Yeah? Where?" He unhanded her and reached across the table to pull the box of doughnuts in front of her.

"Boston."

"I'm from Boston, too. Here." He tipped the box toward her. "The jelly-filled ones are outstanding."

"Yeah, but I'm a sucker for powdered sugar." Sally plucked a powdered doughnut out of the box and took a bite.

Tom chose a jelly doughnut. He sat so close to her that their arms brushed. She breathed in a seductive mingling of bakery sweetness, warm skin and sea air. "You never answered my question," he said. "Are you married?"

Sally's mouth was full. She raised her left hand and wagged the fingers, all bare.

"Oh, yeah. I never think to look there. Seems so…furtive, when you could just ask."

Sally coughed again. "I'm fine," she said in response to his look of concern. "The powdered sugar tickled my throat."

He took a giant bite out of the doughnut. Raspberry jelly oozed from it. He caught a blob on his finger before it fell off, and slid it into his mouth. "How old are you?"

Sally swallowed her bite of doughnut with some difficulty. "Anyone ever tell you you ask a heck of a lot of personal questions?"

"Yeah." He licked some jelly out of the doughnut, took another bite and washed it down with a swallow of coffee. "So, how old are you?"

She grinned and shook her head. "Twenty-six. You?"

"Twenty-nine. I figured you probably weren't married. And I take it there's no, like, live-in boyfriend type situation. 'Cause if there'd been a guy with you when I was sneaking around before, he'd have been the one to come and check things out. Least, I would have hoped so."

"Maybe there *is* a boyfriend," she said, "and I just left him back in Boston."

He shook his head decisively. "No man in his right mind would let a woman like you go off without him for a whole month."

A woman like me? Heat bloomed in Sally's cheeks.

"So this is a vacation for you?" he asked.

"Yep. I love the beaches here. I grew up on Cape Cod Bay."

"You mean you summered here, right?" he said. "Old money, private schools, July and August on the Cape?"

"Do I look like old money to you?"

"If you mean green and wrinkled, no. If you mean elegant in a nice, understated, not-trying-too-hard kind of way, absolutely."

Sally's blush heated to a red-hot glow. "If I'm old money, how come I'm spending August here instead of…I don't know, Saint-Tropez?"

"New money goes to Saint-Tropez. Old money goes to the Cape." He nodded toward the house. "I gotta tell you, though, this wouldn't be my summer home of choice if *I* were filthy stinking rich."

Maybe not, Sally thought, but compared to the modest little bungalow she'd grown up in, this place was Buckingham Palace. She stole a couple of glances at Tom as he polished off another jelly doughnut. He had a symmetrical, well-carved look to him, as if some fastidious sculptor had wanted to create a prototype of the ideal Manly Man—broad forehead, straight nose, square jaw, solid neck, everything balanced and just so. Even his ears were kind of good-looking. His hair was deep brown, almost black, and it curled up quite a bit considering it was pretty short.

Sally froze when Tom turned and reached toward her chest. He lightly brushed a little powdered sugar off her T-shirt. She cleared her throat. "They're kind of messy, powdered doughnuts."

He smiled. "Some of the best things in life are."

She studied her coffee cup. "So, listen. Speaking of sneaking around, as you put it. You really never did tell me why you forced open that glass door."

"Oh. Well, I have to check out the entire house, and since you weren't here yet—or so I thought—I figured I'd just let myself in."

"Check it out?"

"See what needs to be done. Take measurements, order supplies..."

"For what?"

"Phil didn't tell you he was going to have the house fixed up?"

"No."

Tom chuckled. "It can't have escaped your notice that the place is kind of a disaster. Phil said it was run-down even before the hurricane, but now it's virtually unrentable."

"I'm renting it."

"He said you were family and he didn't have to impress you."

"Sounds like Phil."

"And also that you'd be overseeing my work."

"Your work?"

"He hired me to fix up the house," Tom said. "I'm going to live upstairs while I'm doing it, and hopefully finish it up by the end of the month. You're to approve any major renovations and sign off on costs. He didn't tell you any of this?"

"No." Sally sighed. "That's what you do? Repairs and the like?"

"You saw my truck, right?"

"Yeah. What's a spoose?"

He smiled. "It stands for Silk Purses out of Sows' Ears. It's what I call my business."

"Your business? You mean, like a company, with an office and employees and stuff?"

"Nah, it's a one-man show, and I guess my truck is my office. Mostly I work out of Boston, but this month's the exception. I fix stuff up."

"Ah."

"Something wrong?"

"No, I just…no."

"It's the noise and the mess, right? Everybody hates it—all the banging and sawing. All you wanted was a quiet month on the Cape to veg out and along comes messy old Tom O'Hearn tearing things up and scattering dust."

She couldn't help but return his smile. "Something like that, I guess."

"I could try and stay out of your hair," he said. "Wait till you're not around to work in your part of the house, that kind of thing."

"That won't be necessary," she said quickly—too

quickly. "I mean, the mess doesn't bother me that much."

"Glad to hear it." She stopped breathing when he reached a hand out to stroke her face along the edge of her mouth. His fingertips came away smudged with powdered sugar, and he licked them. "Like I said, some of the best things in life are messy."

2

TOM WATCHED HER from the upstairs deck as she walked up the road from the beach, a paperback in one hand and a bright pink beach towel in the other. He tried not to be too obvious in his perusal, checking her out covertly as he pried a rotted two-by-six up from its supports. It was impossible not to look, though.

Bony? Not in that purple crocheted bikini, she wasn't. About a mile and a half of legs, slim but curvy hips, high, petite breasts and nicely lithe arms, all moving in an easy, swaying, very feminine stride—no mean feat in those big old orange flip-flops. Her chin-length hair, now damp and held off her face with sunglasses pushed on top of her head, was the kind of sun-gilded blond you couldn't fake with peroxide. She was pretty in a quirky way, her high cheekbones and generous mouth—and those bottomless, sea green eyes—making up somewhat for a slightly longish nose and chin.

During the three days since they'd taken up residence together in Phil Owen's beach house, Tom had actually seen very little of Sally—except when they joined the rest of the crowd that congregated on the beach at the end of every day to watch the sunset. She spent her mornings on the beach, her afternoons riding her bike and her evenings downstairs in her half of the house. He never heard her TV; he supposed she read. The house commanded most of Tom's time and attention, but more and more, as he sawed and nailed, he found himself wishing she'd wander by so he could strike up a conversation with her.

Right from the beginning, the chemistry between them had been incendiary. The question on Tom's mind was not whether she felt it, too—how could she not?—but whether she was willing to acknowledge it. If he made overtures of a more than friendly nature, would she welcome them or treat him to the dreaded let's-just-be-friends speech? Tom had never pretended to understand women, and for the past couple of years he'd been too busy to even try. He'd forgotten how to strike up a relationship, and she was, after all, a client, more or less. Common sense dictated that he keep his eyes and hands to himself and just do the job he was being paid to do.

At the edge of the sandy yard, she kicked off her sandals and leaned over to pick them up, treating him to a heart-stopping view of the upper slopes of her perfect little hand-size breasts.

Then again, what was common sense but the refuge of soulless middle managers?

The board came loose with a squeal of splitting wood. Tom tossed it over the side onto the pile he'd been accumulating down below, pulled off the bandanna tied over his head and wiped his face and bare chest with it; it came away sodden. Grabbing the sports bottle perched on the deck railing, he squeezed a long, cool stream of water into his mouth.

He leaned on the railing as Sally crossed the side yard. "Careful where you walk," he warned.

"Yeah, this poison ivy's got to go," she said, dodging the tangled patch that surrounded the swing set. "Will you be taking care of that, too?"

"No, Phil said he arranged for a landscaping service to tear it out—sometime this week, I think. But I wasn't talking about the poison ivy. I meant there might be nails."

"Yikes!"

Tom squirted some more water into his mouth. "Did you have a nice swim?"

Pausing on the other side of the pile of weathered boards, she smiled up at him. "Yeah, it was great."

She took another step toward the house, but Tom halted her progress by saying, "If it's not too much trouble, I've got an estimate I need you to approve." He reached into the back pocket of his cutoffs and unfolded the paper napkin on which he'd jotted down the projected cost of pressure-treated lumber for the two new decks.

"I approve it." She stepped onto the lower deck. He could see her by looking down through the gap he'd created by tearing off the old decking.

Crouching over the gap, he said, "You haven't even looked at it."

She peered up at him and shrugged. "I'm sure it's fine." A drop landed on her cheek and she wiped it off. He was sweating on her. Well, if that didn't charm her socks off, nothing would.

"Sorry. Occupational hazard." Tom set the bottle aside, repocketed the napkin, wrapped his hands around a couple of support struts and lowered himself through the gap, landing lightly on his feet right in front of Sally.

She gave him a quick once-over. "Do you always sweat like that when you work?"

"When it's high noon in August, I do. They say the more you sweat, the more efficient your body is at cooling itself down."

"You must be very healthy," she observed with a wry grin as she reached for the sliding glass door.

"There are two sets of numbers," he persisted, withdrawing the paper napkin again. "The first is based on just rebuilding the decks as they were before. The second takes into account some improvements I'd like to make. I was thinking of maybe enlarging both decks, especially the ground floor—"

"Okay."

"Okay?"

She turned to face him. "Okay."

"Don't you think you're being a little cavalier with your cousin's money?" he asked.

Sally tugged at the door, but it wouldn't budge on its corroded runners. "He was a little cavalier when he volunteered me to supervise your work without even consulting me." She yanked at the door. It shifted slightly, but refused to open.

"Allow me." Tom gave the edge of the glass door a few good whacks with the heel of his hand and lifted it out of its frame.

"Uh...will you be able to get that back in?" she asked as she entered her living room.

"I'll do you one better—I'll replace it with a new one. I can do it today if this is a standard-size door. Here." Leaning the door against the side of the house, he tugged his tape measure out of his front pocket, slid the flexible metal tape out of its housing and held the end toward her. "Would you mind?"

She dumped her towel and book on the telephone table and took hold of the tape measure.

"Just hold it right up here," he said, positioning her hand so that she was pressing the tape to the top inner edge of the door frame. "Right there. Don't move."

Kneeling, he noted the measurement to the bottom of the frame, slid his stubby pencil from his back pocket and recorded the number on the napkin. From this perspective, Sally was all legs. Tom breathed in a salty, coconutty fusion of seawater and sunscreen. A fine glitter of sand adhered to her knees; he resisted the urge to brush it off.

"So, do your parents still summer on the Cape?" he asked, just to say something.

"They never did," she said. "Well, they did, but they also wintered, falled and springed. I grew up in the most humble of circumstances, I assure you."

"Get outa here." He repositioned the tape and took the horizontal measurement.

"Our house was this Lilliputian bungalow on the beach. My brother slept in a walk-in closet. I got a tattered couch in the, quote, living room, unquote."

Tom grinned and recorded the number. "I slept on a pullout couch, too—in the basement." He retracted the tape and slid it back in his pocket.

"It wasn't a pullout, and we didn't have a basement." Her gaze seemed to focus on him a little more pointedly. "You slept in the basement?"

"It was a finished basement," he admitted, feeling an absurd pinch of shame to have enjoyed such relative affluence. "But I had to share the pullout couch with my brother. One of them. Three other brothers shared a bedroom, and my four sisters shared another. So, actually, Sean and I had more space and privacy than any of them."

Sally's brow creased. "That's one-two-three-four-five brothers and—"

"There were nine of us." Tom sat on the edge of the picnic table. "Plus my parents. In a six-room South Boston shotgun."

"Shotgun."

"You know. One of those narrow little row houses where you can shoot a shotgun through the front door all the way into the backyard."

She leaned against the door frame. "Lap of luxury. We had only three rooms."

"For how many people?"

"My parents, my brother and me. Four."

"Sorry, ma'am, but according to Hoyle, eleven people in six rooms beats out four people in three for sheer in-your-face, breathin'-my-air crowdedness."

"Hoyle?"

"Isn't that the guy who says what a full house is?"

Sally made a sound halfway between a groan and a chuckle. She had one of those gigantic, toothy smiles that you can't look at without breaking out into a big, goofy smile of your own. Infectious, that was the word for it.

And maybe just a little flirtatious.

She bit her lip and regarded him speculatively for a moment. Finally she said, "Are you hungry?"

"You have no idea."

"I thought I'd open a can of tuna, and it makes too much for just one, so I thought maybe—"

"Count me in." Tom followed her into the house, grinning like a schoolboy.

SALLY WAS AWAKENED from a deep sleep that night by the persistent ringing of the phone. According to the bedside clock, it was just past four a.m. Groaning, she got out of bed and made her way in the dark to the living room. She sank into the battered club chair next to the telephone table, lifted the receiver and nestled it against her ear. "Hello, Amber."

"Sally! Hi! Guess what. Jimmy's first stand-up gig was tonight, and it went great! You should have been there!" Sally's favorite cousin was even more preternaturally chipper than usual tonight.

"What time is it in California?" Sally asked, yawning.

"What? Oh…it's a little after one here. So it's like, what, a couple of hours earlier there?"

"Three hours later, actually."

"Sorry, did I wake you? You should have been there, Sal. You should have seen him. I was so proud of him!"

Sally rubbed her forehead, trying to digest this. "People actually laughed?" Jimmy Lopopolo was the World's Unfunniest Comic—or rather, would-be comic. He wrote arcane, convoluted material, which he delivered in the tranquilizing monotone of an undertaker. Desperate to break into stand-up, he'd talked Amber into moving to L.A. last winter so he could try out in the clubs there.

"One of them laughed," Amber said.

"One of them?"

"There were only two guys in the audience by the time Jimmy went on," Sally's cousin explained. "They'd been sitting together doing shots of tequila all night. One of them was just *howling*. The other probably would have been, but he was sort of out cold."

"Uh-huh. Listen, Amber, has Jimmy given any thought yet to throwing in the towel?"

"Bite your tongue!" Amber scolded. "He'll make it—I know he will."

"What if he doesn't? Do you want to be waiting tables in that demeaning little cowgirl uniform the rest of your life?"

"Demeaning?"

"You told me the skirt came halfway up your thighs."

Amber chuckled. "I hemmed it even shorter a couple of weeks ago, and now I get better tips."

Sally groaned.

"Look," Amber said, "I know you think we're spinning our wheels out here. You thought I was nuts to marry Jimmy in the first place."

"Not nuts."

"You thought I was a traitor."

Yes. "No. You mustn't think that."

"But it's true," Amber said. "We'd made a pact, and I broke it. Now you're the last holdout, and you feel like I've deserted you—abandoned the true cause."

Fifteen years ago, when Sally and Amber were both fourteen, they'd sat together behind a potted palm at their aunt Mary Pat's wedding, sipping from a screwdriver they'd talked an older cousin into ordering for them. Their mothers and their many aunts were lined up on the dance floor for the Electric Slide alongside their husbands. It was the husbands who'd provided grist for the girls' semi-inebriated musings....

"It's like a convention of losers and wanna-bes," Sally had uncharitably observed.

"Too cruel!" Amber replied with a giggle.

"Too true. I mean, I love them, but check it out. There's Uncle Max, the scheme-aholic. What's his big plan this week?"

"I overheard him telling Mom about this chain of tattoo parlors he wants to put in all the malls if he can only get financing."

"That'll happen. And look at Uncle Joe, trying to make a living emptying cesspools in an area that's been hooked up to the sewers for years."

"Did you see his truck in the parking lot? What he painted on the side? My Wife Keeps Her Nose Out Of My Business."

Sally shuddered. "And what about Uncle Dick, the psychic, and Uncle Mike, who's been unemployed and 'finding himself' for, like, seventeen years?"

"Don't forget my dad," Amber said. "He just reapplied to be a CIA agent for, like, the hundredth time."

"What about *my* dad—the only handyman in the United States of America with a master's degree in philosophy. But he gets to live right on the beach, and that's good enough for him."

"What is it about the women in our family?" Amber asked as she tossed back the last of the drink. "Are we all condemned to marry guys with no ambition, no future? Guys who drive cesspool trucks to weddings?"

"Not me!" Sally declared. "And not you, either. You've got to promise me it'll never happen to you."

"Let's make a pact," Amber said. "A blood oath."

"Eewww. Can't we just solemnly swear, like, with our hands over our hearts and stuff?"

Amber sighed. "It won't be the same thing."

"Close enough."

"Deal."

And so they'd sworn, with half-drunken gravity, never to accept a marriage proposal from anyone other than a "successful professional with a steady income and a bitchin' car."

"And he has to be cute," Amber had added as an afterthought.

"That's a given."

Only, Amber had violated their pact by marrying Jimmy, the deadpan professional student turned aspiring comic. Sally had logged countless hours trying to talk her out of it, but it was hopeless; Amber was in love. When Sally had reminded her of their motto, *It's as Easy to Fall in Love with a Rich Man as with a Poor Man*, her cousin's response had been that she couldn't help falling in love with Jimmy; it had just happened.

Well, it'll never "just happen" to me, Sally had silently vowed to herself as she'd toasted Amber and Jimmy's nuptials with the first of too many glasses of champagne. *You can only fall in love with the wrong guy if you let yourself. I just won't let myself.*

Amber's voice jarred Sally out of her reverie. "You're not drifting off to sleep, are you?"

"No," Sally said through a yawn.

"You're probably thinking about how weak I was, and promising yourself you'll hold out for some suit with six figures and a Volvo."

"Was not," Sally lied.

"Were so," Amber countered. "Not that I blame

you. I'm the one who made the pact with you in the first place. Only sometimes love has a way of coming up and biting you on the butt when you least expect it."

"Anyone ever tell you you're a hopeless romantic?"

"Speaking of romance, any new candidates on the horizon?"

Sally instantly thought of Tom O'Hearn wiping powdered sugar off her face. *Some of the best things in life are messy.* "Not really," she hedged.

Amber laughed. "Who is he?"

Sally rolled her eyes. "Nobody."

"Come on, spill!"

"Nobody, just...there's this guy here, fixing up the house."

"A handyman?"

"More of a contractor. And it's just that he's..."

"Cute?"

"Magnificent. About six-two, shoulders out to there and a smile that makes my insides start to hum."

"*Yes!*"

"No. He fixes stuff up for a living—his own words. He works out of his truck, for heaven's sake."

"So? I'm not saying you have to get fitted for a wedding gown. But he sounds like a total babe."

"I won't pretend I'm not interested. The fact is, I fell pretty much helplessly in lust with this guy within minutes of meeting him. And, unless I'm completely delusional, the attraction goes both ways."

"Outstanding! He sounds like he might be just what Safe Sally needs."

"Safe Sally?"

"Admit it, your life is totally colorless. You've carved out this tame, predictable, secure little world for yourself. A tenured teaching job, risk-free investments, that dreary little Back Bay apartment—"

"It's affordable."

"—Those tedious boyfriends with their beige suits and their beige cars and their beige personalities."

"Tell me what you really think," Sally said wryly. "I can take it."

"I really think you ought to enlist Mr. Shoulders-out-to-there—"

"Tom."

"You ought to enlist Tom for a little red-hot summer fling."

Sally chewed on her lip. "I'm not the fling type." Her few serious boyfriends had been undemanding, gentlemanly. They'd respected her desire to take things at a reasonable pace—one Amber liked to refer to as "glacial." But getting intimate with men was inherently risky, and Sally wasn't a risk taker. Although she'd been sexually experienced since her junior year of college, she'd never dreamed of encouraging a man to pursue her for purely sexual reasons.

"I know," Amber said. "That's exactly why you should do it."

"But what if it starts getting serious?"

"You mean what if you can't help falling in love?" Amber asked in her best butter-wouldn't-melt voice. "What if it just happens?"

"Touché. Okay, so it won't get heavy from my end, but what if it gets heavy from his?"

"Men aren't like us," Amber assured her. "Trust me, if you offer this guy a friendly little summer romp with no emotional involvement, he'll jump at the opportunity. Go for it—it'll make your vacation that much more fun."

"Or that much more messy and complicated."

"Hey—no guts, no glory."

"I don't want glory. I want a beige Volvo, remember?"

An extended sigh crackled over the phone line. "All right. Fine. But mark my words—if this guy is as yummy as he sounds, and he's genuinely interested in you, and you burn him off, you're gonna kick yourself afterward."

She's right. "You're wrong."

"You're a coward."

"Duly noted."

3

SALLY HEARD HIM as she glided her bike to a stop on the road in front of the house—or rather, she heard his nail gun discharging about every five seconds. The muffled cracks came from the upper level of the house. He was back at work on the upstairs deck, after a two-day hiatus during which he'd put in new doors and windows—except the front door, which only needed painting—and replaced a few loose cedar shingles.

He was a dynamo, working nonstop every day from dawn until sunset, when, by unspoken agreement, they strolled down to the beach together. Tom had an easy way about him, and struck up conversations with whoever was standing nearby—young families, elderly couples, giggling teenage girls. He seemed to be a magnet for children. The older ones liked to play Frisbee with him. The younger ones begged for him to hoist them on his shoulders and walk them out into the bay, shallow from low tide.

Sally wheeled her bike over the sandy lot and was hauling it up the front stoop when she heard Tom call her name. Backing up a couple of steps, she saw him leaning over the railing of the upper deck at the side of the house. The breath actually left her lungs at the sight of him—Michelangelo's *David* in cutoff army fatigues and bandanna, sun-bronzed and glistening with sweat. She saw the masculine appreciation in his eyes as he smiled down at her, and no wonder; her Lycra bike shorts and cropped T were nearly as revealing as a swimsuit.

"You want to do me a favor and bring me up my level?" he asked. "I've got a short one up here, but I need the long one. It's in the back of my truck. It's kind of like this bar—" he spread his arms "—with these little glass thingamabobs—"

"Yeah, I know what a level looks like," she said. "Give me a second." She stashed her bike inside, yanked off her helmet and checked out her reflection on the microwave, fluffing up her flattened hair. Primping again! *You've got a bad case of Tom O'Hearn, kiddo.*

She climbed into the back of his S•P•O•O•S•E truck, packed with equipment and supplies.

"It's in the big red toolbox," he called out. "That's the one."

Sally shivered under his penetrating gaze as she unlatched the box and sorted through its contents for the level, holding her breath against the oily, metallic toolbox smell, which swept her right back to her childhood. She found the level and squinted up at him. "What are you standing on?" she asked; he seemed to have ripped up all the planking from the deck.

"The support struts."

"You're going to fall through there and hurt yourself."

"Then you'll have to play nurse and kiss my boo-boos." He grinned devilishly. "Might almost be worth it."

She rolled her eyes, but thought, *It might, at that.*

"You can come up the back stairway," he said. "The poison ivy's gone." The landscape crew had worked the place over yesterday.

In back of the house Sally discovered that Tom had already rebuilt the outdoor stairway that led to the upstairs deck; the steps felt rock solid beneath her tread. He'd gotten the first few yards of the narrow deck floored with fresh lumber, and it was a neat job. "Nice work."

"Why, shucks. You're makin' me blush." He took the level from her, laid it on the newest section of flooring and peered at the little bubble. "Bingo." Standing, he said, "Sometimes I think I'm too much of a perfectionist. I could work faster if I let some of the details slide."

"You work pretty fast already. I can't believe the progress you've made in just—what? Five, six days? You should take some time off one of these days, explore the Cape a little bit. Take that fancy bike of yours out for a spin. There are bike trails all over. I'm going to drive up to Provincetown on the tip of the Cape tomorrow and bike through the dunes—it's incredible terrain."

"I can't afford the time for stuff like that. I've only got till the end of August to get everything done." Tom hefted a two-by-six from a stack against the house and positioned it on the struts.

"Why? Does Phil have someone renting the house in September?"

"Nah, he said the place would be empty after we leave." Tom grabbed his nail gun and secured the board with a few quick shots. "The deadline has to do with Phil's timetable for choosing a contractor to renovate the Livermore Building." Tom slammed another board into place next to the other one.

"All right, now you've lost me." Sally sat cross-legged on the new part of the deck. "What's the Livermore Building?"

"Only one of the most important landmark buildings in Boston." *Bam, bam, bam.* With every squeeze of the trigger, Tom's arm muscles jumped. "It's very old and absolutely beautiful, but in pretty sad shape. You didn't know Phil had bought it?"

"To be honest, I don't know Phil all that well. I'm really close to his sister, Amber—she's been my best friend since, like, forever—but Phil and I only see each other at weddings and funerals. He's a New Yorker now, and I've lived in Boston since college."

Tom nailed another board down. "Would you hand me the level?"

"Here, I'll do it." Sally slid the instrument over the new boards and leaned forward to check it. "A-okay."

"A woman of hidden talents." His mouth quirked. "So, if you and Phil are so out of touch, how'd you end up renting this place from him?" He shoved another board in place and nailed it.

"I called Phil in June to thank him for giving my brother a job in his ad agency. Ben's kind of...well, he's had a pretty checkered employment history. A little of this, a little of that—low-level publishing jobs, a job selling radio advertising, some copywriting. He never held a job longer than a year, and he just became more and more unemployable with each ridiculous new resumé."

"Not everyone's cut out for that nine-to-five grind." Tom snugged another board against the last one and reached for his water bottle. "I'm sure not. I like my independence. I'd rather lug around a tool kit than a briefcase any day." He sounded so much like Sally's father that, for a moment, all she could do was stare at him.

Mentally shaking herself, she said, "Anyway, Phil offered Ben some really great position—account executive, I think. I still can't figure out why. I mean, he'd always liked Ben—they used to goof around a lot when they were kids—but Ben isn't qualified to answer the phones at that agency."

"If I had to wager a guess, I'd say Phil's paying Ben probably half what he'd have to pay a real account executive, someone with experience. He's quite the skinflint, your cousin. Criminally cheap." Tom took a drink from his water bottle.

"Is he paying you fairly for your work on this house?"

"Not really, but this house is kind of a special project. It's all tied in to the Livermore Building."

"Ah, yes." Sally leaned against the side of the house and stretched her legs out. "The Livermore Building."

Tom's gaze lingered on her legs as he wiped his mouth with the back of his hand. "Want some?" He offered the bottle to Sally.

She hesitated.

"Nothing communicable, I swear." He captured her gaze and smiled. "Totally clean bill of health."

Sally had been blundering around in the singles scene long enough to recognize that declaration for what it was—a qualification for courtship, same as good looks, a swell car or a high-status occupation. Tom had the looks, all right; no declarations needed.

He had the health, if he was to be believed. Unfortunately, his car was a truck with S•P•O•O•S•E painted on the side, and as for his occupation...

He took her hand and wrapped it around the bottle, his calluses grazing her, his tone inveigling, almost intimate. "Come on, I know you want some."

Sally took the bottle and squeezed water into her mouth, feeling self-conscious under his gaze. She wasn't used to men looking at her quite as intensely as Tom did. It made her feel shivery and hot at the same time.

"So you called Phil to thank him for underpaying your brother." Tom aimed the nail gun. *Bam, bam, bam.*

"Better that than unemployment. Anyway, during the course of the conversation, Phil asked me if I knew anyone who might want to rent the bottom half of his beach house for the month of August, and I said yeah, me—if the price was right."

Tom slammed another board in place. "He should pay *you* to live here."

"Oh, it's not so bad." She checked the newly laid boards with the level. "So, what's the deal with the Livermore Building?"

"Your cousin bought it to house a satellite of his agency, which I take it is based in Manhattan."

"Phil Owen and Associates. It's grown amazingly since Phil founded it. He's won two Clios."

"Groovy. Well, he's expanding into Boston, and apparently he wanted the cachet of the Livermore Building, but without the dry rot and rusty plumbing. He took bids recently. Mine had to be the lowest one, or just about, but my goal isn't to turn a profit—I might even lose money on the deal. See, right now my business is pretty new, and it's still on shaky ground."

Shaky ground? Losing money? If this guy was trying to get over with her, Sally reflected, he had a funny way of doing it.

"I'm trying to specialize in the renovation of historic buildings," he continued. "I've handled a few small jobs, but nothing on the scale of the Livermore. If I pull that one off, and do it right, it'll establish my reputation. It's a golden opportunity for me, and I mean to capitalize on it."

"Okay—but what does the Livermore Building have to do with this house?"

"Phil's gonna be picking a contractor the first week of September. I know he's leaning toward hiring me. Problem is, all the other guys who put bids in have years more experience than I do—all in general contracting, not historic renovation, but still. I know Phil's kind of hesitant to sign me on. He offered me this job to see what I'm capable of. If I can whip this baby into shape in a month, the Livermore job is mine."

"No wonder you're such a workaholic."

"Oh, I always am. It's my cross to bear." Tom positioned another board. He had to shift around to get into a position where he could nail it, but it was an easy reach for Sally. She lifted the nail gun and aimed it.

Tom frowned. "You ever handle one of those?"

"When I was a kid."

"A *kid?*" His surprise was understandable. Nail guns could be lethal.

"Sure." She aimed the gun over the part of the

board that was resting on the strut. "Fisher Price makes 'em—'My First Nail Gun.'"

"Get outa here."

She laughed. "You *believed* that?"

A pink stain tipped his ears, but he smiled. "A woman like you could tell a guy just about anything and he'd believe it."

A woman like you. That was the second time he'd referred to her that way. Sally squeezed the trigger three times, driving three nails through the board and into the strut.

Tom rubbed the nail heads with his fingertips. "Nice job."

Sally blew into the barrel of the gun, like a Wild West gunslinger. "Quickest draw on the Cape."

"No, really. You *do* have hidden talents."

She smiled impishly. "Are you trying to make me blush?"

He leaned toward her, his voice lowering. "Do you want me to make you blush?"

She chuckled nervously. "You think you have that kind of power?"

"You seem to blush pretty easily. Must be your coloring." He drew her into his earnest blue gaze and held her there. "And when you do blush, you look incandescent—I mean, even more than usual, and that's saying something."

Heat stung her cheeks.

"The pink in your skin—" he trailed his fingertips over her face "—makes your eyes incredibly green, like emeralds. And your lips get bright red." He grazed her lower lip with a thumb that felt like fine-grade sandpaper, raising blissful little goose bumps all over her. "And hot."

Sally swallowed hard, her face scalding.

"What do you know." He smiled slowly. "Looks like I do have the power."

"A parlor trick," she said airily—or it might have seemed airy if her voice had been steadier. "All women blush when they're complimented."

"Not like you do, which leads me to think you don't get complimented nearly as often as you deserve."

"I'll have to chastise my many adoring suitors next time I see them."

"Sarcasm? You mean there's a dearth of adoring suitors? A woman like you should have men groveling at her—"

"*A woman like me* isn't what most men fantasize about when the lights go out."

Tom burst out laughing. "Hate to contradict you, but leggy blond cover-model types are pretty much guaranteed to jump-start any male with a pulse."

"'Leggy' being a euphemism for 'gawky.'"

"If 'gawky' means you're the kind of woman men gawk at, I'd have to agree with you."

She rolled her eyes. "I'm six feet tall, Tom. Six. Feet."

"Outstanding. If we were married, we could borrow each other's clothes."

Sally choked on her tongue.

"I'm moving a little too fast, aren't I?"

She found her voice, or a croaky semblance thereof. "You were on cruise control for a while there, but I'd say you've just shifted into hyperspace."

"You're thinking I'm some kind of smooth operator."

She cocked an eyebrow. "Not smooth."

"Ouch." He rubbed the back of his neck, his expression sheepish. "I'm usually not this... Actually, I'm never this..."

"Obvious?"

"Interested." He met her gaze. "I mean, I like women, but I'm not some kind of Casanova. My work, it's pretty demanding. I've spent the past couple of years trying to get my business going, and it hasn't left a lot of room for a social life. Or interest in one, if you want to know the truth. All I've cared about was getting S•P•O•O•S•E off the ground."

"You don't date much?"

"Closest I've come lately was my sister Bridget's wedding reception last December. One of the bridesmaids—Mary Katherine Flaherty, I think her name was—she got to feeling frisky and dragged me into the janitor's closet at the VFW hall."

"Ah, romance."

"Both of us ended up with skinned knees from the concrete floor, and her palms were all—"

"That's a little more detail than I probably need."

"What I'm trying to say is, I don't mean to be coming on so strong here, but it's almost like I can't help it. You're the first woman who's really spun my wheels in a long time, and I guess I've forgotten how to be subtle. But I'm not a complete Neanderthal, and I don't want to ruin your vacation if I've misread the signals or something. I mean, if that's the case, there's a shower in back of the house with all the cold water a boy in my position could need. If you want me to back off, just say the word."

Sally looked away from the intensity of his gaze,

her lower lip caught between her teeth. *No guts, no glory.*

"You're not saying anything," he said quietly.

She opened her mouth to speak, but nothing came out. *Coward.*

He moved closer to her, his gaze locked on hers. "Let me guess. You're at least a little bit interested...nod if I'm getting warm."

She nodded.

"But you're not used to things moving this fast. I can understand that. But it feels right, doesn't it?"

Sally nodded again. Did it ever. Maybe Amber was right. Maybe a little red-hot summer fling was just what she needed. The prospect both thrilled and unnerved her.

"I'm dying to kiss you," Tom said, his gaze focusing on her mouth. "Just a little kiss, just to kind of break the ice."

A nervous chuckle bubbled out of Sally. After a brief hesitation, she nodded. Tom's eyes lit with anticipation. He leaned forward. So did Sally. She closed her eyes, and then came the delicious heat of his mouth grazing hers. The heat spread through her, filling her with a kind of languid desire. His lips were surprisingly soft, the kiss lingering and gentle and reassuring, as he'd surely meant it to be. It was a kiss that said, *I'm going to do this right. I'm willing to take my time. I'm not going to throw you on your back and rip your clothes off and devour you...*

"Not yet," he murmured against her lips.

"What?" Sally broke the kiss, startled.

"Sorry." He rubbed his neck. "Just talking to myself. You seem a little skittish, so I want to make sure I don't move too fast and spoil things."

Sally cleared her throat; her lips felt ticklish, as if they wanted more. Now. But all she said was, "Thank you." If he was willing to take this one step at a time, that would be for the best. She didn't know if she could deal with going from zero to sixty with a man she hardly knew.

He glided a fingertip along the edge of her jaw, over her chin and down her throat, leaving trails of sensation that made Sally shiver with longing. If he kept up this kind of thing, she'd end up throwing *him* on his back.

"I've got an idea." He smoothed a rough palm over her upper chest above the scoop-necked T-shirt; she wondered if he could feel her rioting heart. "How'd you like to give me a hand rebuilding this deck?"

"Huh?"

He smiled. "An extra pair of hands would make it go faster. If I were to place the boards while you nailed them, that'd save me a couple of hours of work, and then I could afford to take some time off tomorrow. Maybe if I asked you real nice, you'd let me tag along with you to Provincetown."

"Oh." Like a date? she wondered.

"Like a date. I figure it might not be a bad idea if we got away from here and went out and had a little fun together. We could pack a picnic lunch, spend some time talking, get to know each other a little better. What do you say?"

"I guess. Sure. It'd be fun."

"That's the spirit. All right then, Madame Quick-Draw." He lifted a board and thrust it into position. "Ready, aim, fire."

4

"THIS IS REALLY SOMETHING!" Tom called over his shoulder as he pedaled ahead of Sally along the meandering bike trail.

"Like another planet." Sally had always loved this stretch after you came out of the woods, a landscape of undulating dunes and beach brush made all the more otherworldly by the silvery light from the overcast sky. By Sally's watch, it was a little after one in the afternoon, but it looked almost like dawn. It was a strange world they rode through, and silent except for the occasional caw of a seagull circling overhead. "We're coming up to the beach."

"Great. I'm starving."

They'd taken turns riding in front on the narrowest parts of the trail. Spectacular though the scenery was, whenever Sally was behind Tom, she found herself hard-pressed to tear her gaze away from his back, a wedge of concentrated power sloping downward and inward from those mammoth shoulders. Every time he turned or shifted gears, muscles rose and fell beneath his faded maroon T-shirt, dark with sweat in a narrow triangle between his shoulder blades.

The beach opened out in front of them, deserted due to the lack of sun and the unseasonably brisk temperature—great for biking, but not exactly beach

weather. On days like this, everyone on the upper
end of the Cape generally swarmed into quaint little
Provincetown, a former fishing village turned artists'
colony turned tourist trap. Sally would just as soon
be out here, breathing in the cool, salty air and letting
the breeze ruffle her hair.

"Looks like we've got it all to ourselves," Tom observed as they locked up their bikes and unfastened
the packs that held their lunch and a threadbare
plaid blanket Sally had found in one of the closets; it
already had sand in it, so clearly it was intended for
beach service. They unfastened their water bottles
from their bikes and took off their sneakers and
socks.

Sally pointed. "Let's head down that way."

They laid the blanket as close to the incoming
waves as they could get and still have dry sand beneath them. The subject of yesterday's kiss hadn't
come up today, and Tom hadn't attempted a repeat
performance—although, from the hungry way he
gazed at her when he thought she wasn't looking,
she could guess it was on his mind.

As soon as they were settled on the blanket, he
started rooting through the contents of the insulated
bag Sally had packed. "What kind of sandwiches are
these?"

"Roast beef. Hope you're not a vegetarian."

"Nah, I'm your basic caveman. If it's flesh, I'll eat
it. There are three sandwiches here."

"Two are for you."

"I think I love you." He held a hand up. "Just kidding. Whoa—Snickers bars! I take it back, I'm not
kidding. Will you marry me?"

"No."

"Be that way." He handed a sandwich to her and tore open the foil on one of his, devouring half of it in three bites. Seagulls swooped down and settled around them, scrutinizing their every move.

Tom polished off his two sandwiches while Sally was still halfway through hers, then he stretched out on his side to watch her with an expression of indolent contentment. It was the look of a man reclining in bed after an exhausting bout of lovemaking.

"So," he said, "how'd a nice girl like you learn to wield a nail gun with such awesome authority?"

Ah, so he really did want to learn more about her. "I told you," Sally said around a mouthful of sandwich. "I learned as a kid."

"'My First Nail Gun'?" He retrieved the plastic container full of cherries that Sally had packed, popped one in his mouth and tossed the pit into the sand. The seagulls descended on it in a flurry of white feathers. "No, seriously, how'd you learn?"

"Seriously. I learned when I was a kid. Just like I learned to use a level and a drill and a power sander and every kind of saw there is, electric and manual. I can put up drywall, lay ceramic tile, hang wallpaper, repair roofs, you name it. I learned from helping out my father."

"Your father? Is he a contractor, like me?"

"More of a handyman." Still, the similarities between the two men were too unnerving to ignore. Both of them had a truck for an office and worked irregular hours without the remotest prospect of a regular paycheck. Sally ate the last of her sandwich, rolled the foil into a ball and stuck it back into the insulated bag.

"Dad has a master's degree in Eastern philosophy," she said. "He's incredibly smart—maybe even brilliant. But all he wants out of life is to listen to the waves and read his books. A couple of years ago, he and Mom moved to Florida, but they still live right on the beach, and he still supports them with odd jobs." Sally reclined on her side facing Tom. "So, how'd you happen to get into your line of work?"

"I started doing a little bit of it in college, to help out with tuition."

"You went to college?" Sally brought a cherry to her mouth and began nibbling it off the stem.

"I had a football scholarship to Yale."

Sally gulped her cherry pit. "Yale?"

He looked at her, grinning crookedly. "Yeah, it's this school in Connecticut."

"I've heard of it. You played football for Yale?"

"Until I blew out my right knee in my junior year and had to quit the team."

"Oh, no."

"I've had surgery on the knee, and it hardly bothers me at all anymore, but it ruined me for football. In a way, it was a relief, 'cause I had a pretty heavy course load, and during football season, my academics suffered."

"What were you taking?"

"I was in a five-year architecture program, so I had to take math, engineering, mechanical drawing, computer science…" He reached into the container for more cherries. "But once the scholarship money was gone, I couldn't afford it. I had to quit school after my junior year."

"Oh. That's awful."

"I came back to Boston and subcontracted for a few years until it dawned on me that what I really wanted to do was fix up old buildings. It's a crime to let one just crumble away when it can be reconditioned and saved."

Sally chose another cherry. "Silk purses out of sows' ears," she murmured.

"Exactly. You should see my own house. Talk about a sow's ear. It was an estate sale. The old lady who owned it had let it pretty much collapse around her—her and her eleventy-seven cats. That's the only reason I was able to afford it."

"Where is it?"

"Beacon Hill."

"Beacon Hill! Not one of those wonderful old town houses."

"You bet, only it wasn't so wonderful when I first went to work on it. It's taking forever, 'cause I have to do all the work at night after I'm done with my regular jobs. It's starting to come together, though. 'Course, it would help if I could afford furniture, but furniture's overrated."

"Are you planning on reselling it? I'll bet you'd make a tidy profit."

"I'd triple my investment. Quadruple it, maybe, but no. That house is my home. I plan on dying there." Tom withdrew the last cherry and tossed the container into the insulated bag. He held the cherry toward Sally, nudging her lips with it. She plucked it off its stem with her teeth. His gaze lit on her mouth. She saw his throat move as he swallowed. "Your turn now," he said, tossing the stem aside and resting his head in his big hand. "How'd you get into teaching?"

Their knees were touching, she realized. He was close enough so that she felt his body heat and breathed in his clean, sweat-dampened scent. "It seemed like something I could do."

Little creases formed between his brows. "So did modeling, right? You said you modeled in college. Did you like it?"

"Yeah, I guess. It was fun, and there was that aura of glamour."

"Did you ever consider pursuing it?"

"For real? Like moving to New York and getting into print work?"

"I guess."

"Not really. I mean, people used to try and talk me into it, but that kind of work's a crapshoot. If you don't strike it big, you can go a long time between jobs, with nothing to show for it. And not only is the money unreliable, but it's all over by the time most people's careers are just getting off the ground."

"Yeah, but it would have been fun and glamorous. Maybe you should have given it a shot. No guts, no glory."

Déjà vu. "I didn't want glory. I wanted job security. With teaching, the pay's good, and once you're tenured, you're pretty much guaranteed a job."

"Forgive me, but that sounds like pretty cold-blooded motivation to pursue your life's work."

"In the beginning, my decision to teach *was* cold-blooded," Sally admitted. "I'd thought it all out. It was either teaching, nursing or civil service, and I picked teaching. Once I got into it, I realized I loved it. I really relate to high school kids—maybe because I'm not that much older than them. It excites me to expose them to literature and help mold their minds. And I think I've gotten pretty good at it, if I do say so myself."

He smiled. "I'm sure you are. And I'm sure the boys in your classes are completely smitten with you."

"No, they aren't."

"No? You didn't tell me you taught at a school for the blind."

"Har har."

He lowered his voice to a seductive, European-accented purr. "You're enchanting when you laugh, *chérie*. But not when you go, 'Har har.'"

She did laugh then, for real.

"That's better. What an outstanding smile you've got." He traced her lips with a fingertip. "The cherries stained your lips red."

Tom studied her lips, which tingled beneath his whispery touch, then looked up and met her gaze. His eyes glowed like blue fire in this eerie light.

He tilted her chin up slightly and her heart raced. She closed her eyes just for a moment, to get her bearings. When she opened them, his face was very close to hers. The rise and fall of his chest mirrored her own ragged breathing, in contrast to the slow and steady hush of the waves.

"I'd really like to kiss you again," he said.

She smiled, although she felt absurdly nervous. "I'd like that, too."

He curled his hand around her neck, urging her infinitesimally closer. "A real kiss this time. Like I mean it."

"Tom—"

"'Cause I do."

"Tom, you really don't need to ask. Just—"

His mouth closed over hers hungrily, almost violently, while he gripped the back of her head to draw her closer. They wrapped their arms around each other, their bodies fusing, their legs intertwined. It was as if their mutual longing, having been kept at bay for a week, had suddenly detonated. The impact rocked Sally to her core.

Tom rolled on top of her, his weight on his elbows, his hands in her hair, and relaxed the kiss, easing the pressure of his mouth on hers. His lips were soft in contrast to the raspy skin surrounding them, and warm, and so achingly gentle that she could barely breathe.

"You taste like cherries," he breathed against her mouth. She felt the hot sweep of his tongue at the seam of her lips, the erotic sense of invasion as it thrust and teased. A current of desire surged within her, sweeping her misgivings before it like a shard of beach glass tossed ashore by the waves.

His lips brushed a feverish path across her mouth to the edge of her chin, which he lightly licked, and over the ultra-sensitive skin on the underside of her jaw. Sally's breath grew quick and shallow as he kissed a tingling trail down her throat and over the soft cotton of her T-shirt. Her nipples tightened; her body strained against his.

Children laughed in the distance; a dog barked. Sally and Tom both looked toward the sound to find a black lab and two young girls running toward the water, with a man and a woman following at a more leisurely pace. The woman turned to look in their direction.

Tom quickly rolled off of Sally and helped her to sit up. "It's just as well," he said. "I was that close to going way too far. Or trying to. And I don't relish the idea of getting my face slapped just when everything's going so well."

"I wouldn't have slapped your face."

"No, but you would have asked me to slow down."

She considered that. "Probably," she admitted. "I'm just not used to everything happening so fast."

"I know, and I promised you I wouldn't push you." After a moment's thought he said, "Just tell me one thing, okay?"

She swallowed. "Sure."

He nodded toward the insulated bag. "Are we gonna eat those Snickers bars or what?"

5

"BASEBALL," Tom announced as he shuffled the deck.

Sally came out of her brand-new kitchen with a blender full of piña coladas and two glasses. "Baseball?"

"Seven-card stud with a few bells and whistles," he explained, dealing the cards onto Sally's dining table while he tried to keep from gaping at her like a schoolboy. He'd never seen her in a skirt until tonight, but apparently she'd decided to dress up for their impromptu party to celebrate the completion of her kitchen. It wasn't a skirt so much as a sarong, a swath of silk in a tropical print that wrapped and tied on the side. It was way too long, of course, but conformed so well to her tight little bottom and mile-high legs that it became a religious experience just to watch her walk across the room. Between the top of the sarong and the bottom of her abbreviated white T-shirt, a strip of flat, tanned stomach, complete with belly button, was just visible. Her skin gleamed with a fine sheen of perspiration; it was a hot night.

"Earth to Tom."

He responded with a sigh.

"I said, what bells and whistles?" Her hip brushed his shoulder as she set a glass in front of him and filled it with the frothy concoction in the blender. A heady fragrance—part pineapple, from the piña colada, and part jasmine, from Sally—tickled his senses.

"Uh…oh. Seven-card stud, threes and nines are wild, if you're dealt a four faceup you get an extra card, if you get the queen of spades faceup the cards are reshuffled and we start over, but if it's facedown you split the pot with the—"

"Whoa there, Diamond Jim." She regarded him with something akin to outrage as she poured her own drink across the table from him. "I just learned how to play regular seven-card stud. Until tonight, I didn't even know how to play five-card draw. And now you expect me to try and remember all that about threes and nines—"

"Three strikes you're out, nine innings to a game. It's easy if you think about baseball."

"I never think about baseball."

"Not even the—"

"Not even the Red Sox."

He slapped his hand over his heart. "Heresy. I can't believe I'm lusting after a woman who doesn't worship the Boston Red Sox."

Almost a week had passed since their kiss on the beach. Six interminable days. Although Tom had made admirable progress in renovating the house— with help from Sally, who really did know how to use a power saw, God bless her—he'd made little headway in the seduction department. He sensed a slight uneasiness in her whenever he tried to go much further than kissing, so that's where they'd plateaued—but it just wasn't enough. Granted, the kissing was great—so great, in fact, that it left him eager for more, sometimes so desperately eager that it was all he could do to back off when he had to. Sexual frustration had achieved agonizing new heights he'd never thought possible.

It sometimes crossed his mind to ask her to stop helping him out with the house, because her constant presence only intensified his desire for her. But how could he send her away when her very nearness made him feel so damn good? She was like a drug, as maddening as she was intoxicating, and impossible to do without.

"Tom?" She was sitting opposite him, her cards in her hand, regarding him curiously. "I said, what's the ante?"

"Oh. Two clams." He sorted through the pile in front of him and dropped two clamshells into the middle; she did the same.

Maybe he was making a mistake by playing the gentleman and backing off all the time. She wasn't unwilling, she was just used to a slower pace of romancing. Problem was, they only had a month together in this house. If he kept retreating every time she seemed a little reluctant, they'd still be at the necking stage by the time they went their separate ways.

"You seem a little distracted tonight," she said.

He lifted his glass, smiling. "To distractions." She clinked her glass against his; he plucked the straw out of the piña colada and downed the drink in one icy tilt. It made him shiver, which felt great on such a stifling night, but then a cold-drink headache kicked in, making him wince.

"Too cold?" Sally asked.

"I think I'm having a stroke," he muttered, rubbing his forehead.

"That's not the only reason to slow down there, big guy. It doesn't taste like it, but there's a lot of rum in there." She inspected her cards. "Remind me— what happens if someone gets the queen of spades faceup?"

He tossed his cards into the middle. "Do-over."

"Oh, yeah," she said morosely. "I had a good hand, though."

"Them's the breaks." He reached for her cards. "Hand 'em over."

She sighed disgruntedly and gave him her cards. "Now you deal them again?"

"I could." He gathered the cards together and tapped them against the table. "Or I could teach you something else."

"Another incredibly Byzantine version of poker?" She lifted her glass to her lips. "Lucky me."

"Forget poker." He slapped the cards down. "You don't like it. You're just humoring me."

"So, what are you planning on teaching me?"

"Something a lot more fun than poker." He smiled slowly as he rose from the table. "But that sarong of yours might just get in the way."

"Uh, Tom…"

"Let's dance."

Her eyes widened. "Uh-uh. No. No way. I don't dance."

"Why not?" He crossed to the sideboard and started flipping through the LPs stacked up next to the battered old record player. "What's your pleasure? You've got your Ronettes, you've got your Jerry Lee Lewis—"

"And I've got a powerful aversion to dancing."

"Wow! Little Richard!" He slid the record from its

sleeve and loaded it onto the turntable. "You don't know how to dance. That's not the same as an aversion."

"It's not that I don't know how. It's that I can't. I'm completely uncoordinated."

"*Au contraire, chérie.*" He turned the record player on and set the needle down. "I've seen you move."

"No, I mean, look at this foot." As Little Richard launched into the high-octane opening of "Tutti Frutti," Sally turned in her chair, slid off her strappy sandal and stuck a bare foot out. The sarong parted, exposing her leg to the top of the thigh.

"You seriously expect me to be looking at your foot?"

She rolled her eyes. Tom squatted down in front of her and took her foot in his hands. "It's a very capable-looking appendage."

"It's a size ten-and-a-half appendage."

"Excellent." He kneaded her instep. "We can share shoes, too."

She cast a jaundiced eye in the direction of his ancient, paint-spattered moccasins. "I think I'll pass. Seriously, though, I can't dance. I literally trip over my own feet sometimes."

"So do I, and I learned how to dance. Big Irish families tend to have lots of weddings. Before each one, my aunts used to give dancing lessons to all the kids." Cradling her foot in one hand, Tom stroked upward, gently massaging her calf. "My thorough examination—and it *is* thorough—reveals no abnormalities of either the foot or leg that should prevent you from executing a perfectly acceptable funky chicken."

"*That's* gonna happen."

"Come on." His massage gravitated to her thigh, which was firm and warm and as smooth as satin. "What have you got to lose but your dignity?"

She pried his hand off her thigh, yanked her sarong closed and slid her foot back into the sandal. "Don't ever go into sales, Tom."

"I think I already knew that." He stood up and offered her his hand. "Come on. I know you want to."

She covered her face with her hands and moaned.

Gripping her shoulders, he lifted her to her feet. "How can you hear music like this and not want to dance?"

"We can't dance in here," she said, indicating her living room with a sweep of her hand. She was right. The new flooring was ideal, but every available square foot was occupied by furniture—new stuff still in plastic, picked out by Sally, charged to Phil's account and delivered that day, and the old stuff, which would be hauled away tomorrow.

"Why don't we do it in the road?" Tom crooned, earning one of Sally's patented arched eyebrows for his troubles. "Or out back. There's plenty of room now." She let him lead her by the hand through the sliding door to the spacious new deck. He shoved the new picnic table, which he'd built from leftover lumber, into a corner against the wall of the house. "Voilà! A dance floor."

It was milder outside, thanks to the breeze off the bay, but still awfully warm for this time of night. The light from within the house cast a soft amber glow onto the deck, burnishing Sally's skin and making her hair gleam like soft fire. Leaning over, she lifted the hem of her sarong and tucked it into the waist, transforming it into a miniskirt. Tom didn't think he'd ever seen anything as unabashedly flat-out excellent to look at as Sally Curran's legs.

Man, you are so far gone, he thought as he placed her left hand on his shoulder and took her right in his. "Tutti Frutti" yielded to "Short Fat Fanny" and "Whole Lot-ta Shakin' Goin' On." By the time the first side was over, he'd taught Sally all the basic steps and combinations she would ever need. She wasn't half-bad, and he even suspected she was enjoying herself. By the time Little Richard started wailing, "Oh, baby...yes, baby...baby...havin' me some fun tonight," she was looking damn good, and laughing to boot.

"That was your song," he told her as she executed a pretty respectable spin at the end. "Long Tall Sally."

"That just about sums me up," she said breathlessly, sinking cross-legged onto the floor as Tom went inside to turn off the record player. "Wow, I worked up a sweat."

Sitting next to her, Tom blotted her face, and then his own, with the hem of his T-shirt. "Sweat is healthy, remember?"

"That's what I hear." She leaned back on her hands, chuckling. "I can't believe you actually taught me how to dance."

"See? It wasn't so hard."

"You're a good teacher," she said.

"You're very graceful."

She laughed. "Yeah, right."

"You are. I love to watch you move. You've got a kind of loose-limbed thing going there."

"Like a marionette."

"Like a gazelle." He reached out to smooth back

her disheveled hair. "You're so beautiful. How can you not know how beautiful you are?" He touched his lips to hers, softly. She tasted salty.

"Sometimes," he said between whisper-light kisses, "I look over at you while we're working on the house, and it's all I can do to keep my hands off of you. All I think about, all day and all night, is how much I want you." He lowered her gently to the deck, lying over her, but resting his weight on his arms. "I imagine what it would be like to take off all your clothes."

"Tom..."

He silenced her protests with a kiss, not a gentle kiss this time, but a deep and demanding one. She couldn't have been that balky, because she wrapped her arms around him. He threaded his fingers through her hair, tilted her head back and kissed her throat. "I want to touch you," he rasped, caressing her hungrily through her clothes. "And kiss all the places I've touched."

He started tugging at the knot that secured her sarong. She hitched in her breath and closed a hand over his.

He took her face in his hands. "I want to be inside you, Sally. I want it all the time. I really do lie awake thinking about you...wondering what it would be like to make love to you. Don't tell me you haven't thought about it, too." In the golden half-light he saw that her cheeks were flushed, her eyes languorous. "I know you have."

"Yes, but...I thought we were going to take things one step at a time."

A smile tugged at his lips. "I've been rethinking

the wisdom of that. Why should we wait when it's what we both want?''

She looked away from his gaze, her brow furrowed.

Tom sat up with his back to her and looked out toward the bay. From the vast darkness surrounding them came the trill of insects in the grassy field and the distant whisper of waves on the beach.

"I shouldn't have tried to force the issue." He closed his eyes and rubbed his neck. "If you're not ready, you're not ready."

When he opened his eyes and looked behind him, Sally was sitting up, her arms around her updrawn knees, watching him. "Tom, I'm—"

"Forget it." He stood and offered her his hand. She took it and rose. "I was impatient. It's my fault."

"Tom—"

"I'm gonna go for a swim." He kicked his moccasins off at the edge of the deck and stepped down into the sand.

"Now? It must be close to midnight."

"Look, I'm sorry for rushing things and making you feel pressured. We can go right back to the way it was before."

"Tom—"

"See you in the morning." He turned and sprinted off toward the beach.

IF YOU'RE NOT READY, you're not ready.

Sally rolled over in bed for the hundredth time, trying in vain to get comfortable enough to sleep. It wasn't any physical discomfort keeping her awake, of course; it wasn't even the warmth of the night, although her room had a tendency to collect heat.

It was Tom.

After a glance at the clock—it was 1:51 a.m.—she got up and walked to the darkened living room. Squinting at the phone, she punched out Amber's number and settled into the club chair.

The fourth ring was interrupted halfway through by Amber growling, "This better be important. I'm in the *middle* of something here."

"Uh…"

"Sally?"

"You recognized my voice from me going 'uh'?"

"Hey, we're soul sisters!" Amber exclaimed, having gone from ticked off to perky in about a second and a half. "Jimmy, wait with that." She laughed breathily. "Wait, Jimmy. It's Sally."

"Am I, uh, interrupting something?"

"Are you ever." Amber gasped. "Yes…I mean, no. Jimmy, sweetie, not now. Here. Have some more champagne."

"Champagne?"

"We're celebrating! Jimmy went out and bought a bottle of champagne, a jar of chocolate body paint and a can of whipped cream. A casting agent saw his act and asked him to come in and read for a sitcom pilot."

"No kidding!"

"Not a huge part, but he'd be on every week. He'd be playing the lead's best friend, this hopeless dreamer type, but a real deadpan character. They wanted someone who could deliver his lines with almost no inflection."

"That's our Jimmy. Wow! How come you didn't tell me this?"

"I was gonna call you, but it's so much earlier there—"

"Later."

"Whatever. And then I got distracted."

"So I see. I can call back tomorrow."

"Don't be silly. I bought us a couple of minutes by pouring him some more champagne. The thing is," Amber confided, lowering her voice, "he's real hard to rein in once he gets started. You'd never think such a low-key guy could be such a *beast* in bed."

"Thank you for sharing that with me."

"So, speaking of male animals," Amber said, "how's it going with the shoulders guy?"

"Tom?"

"Tom. Are you up to speed in the old fling department yet?"

"Actually, we're kind of stuck in low gear. Maybe even neutral."

"Your doing, I assume."

Sally sighed and dragged a hand through her hair.

"You're not still worried that he's gonna ruin everything by getting too serious, are you?" Amber asked. "'Cause I'm telling you, any man would just as soon have the sex without having to romance you."

"I know. That's not it."

"Let me guess," Amber said. "You've been waiting till you're 'ready,' just like with the Beige Brigade."

"I hate you," Sally groaned.

Amber chuckled. "Get with the program, Sal! This is a fling, not a relationship. With relationships, you go from first base to home in the right order, playing strictly by the rules, all nice and comfy and predictable. This process has the advantage of making Safe Sallies feel, well, safe—"

"I hate you *a lot*," Sally elaborated.

"But naturally, there's a giant downside."

"Naturally."

"The game becomes boring," Amber said. "No surprises. And by the time you finally lumber on into home, you've been anticipating it for so long that it's more of a relief than a thrill. Any of this sound familiar to you?"

"You know it does. Have I mentioned that I hate you?"

"The cool thing about flings," Amber continued, "is that you get to throw the rule book away and do whatever feels right at the moment. If the spirit moves you, you can skip second and third base entirely, make a mad dash across the infield and slide right on into home. Now, *that's* a thrill."

"Are you making up this analogy as you go along?"

"Not bad considering I'm getting my toes sucked, so I'm kind of distracted. You want some whipped cream with that, Jimmy? No? He's a purist."

"So you're saying I should...go for the home run right now?"

"No. I'm saying you should've done it days ago. You know, for a bright girl, you're not too bright sometimes."

"Tell me something I don't know."

"Okay. Betcha don't know that Jimmy's given up on my toes and started working his way up my right leg."

"That'd be my cue to hang up."

"That'd be it."

"Thanks for the advice, Amber. And tell Jimmy *bon appétit.*"

Amber answered her with a moan.

Sally replaced the receiver, got up and went out onto the back deck, where she breathed deeply of the mild, brine-scented night air. Although almost two hours had passed since Tom left for his swim, she knew he hadn't come home yet; she'd have heard him on the creaky stairs to the upper level if he had.

The old lawn furniture had already been carted away, so there was no place to sit except for the dilapidated swing set, which still stood in the side yard. Sally hesitated, worried that someone might see her in her nightgown, but not only was the swing set hidden from the road behind a clump of beach plum bushes, the house across the way was vacant except on weekends. And, of course, it was almost 2:00 in the morning; there wasn't a light on as far as she could see in any direction.

She sat on the only remaining swing, a weathered plastic seat that hung close to the ground. Holding on to the rusty chain, she stretched out, snugging her feet into the sand and leaning back to look up into the infinite, inky sky. A full moon hung like a lantern amid a glittery sprinkling of stars. Insects still sang in the untended meadow, accompanied by the slow, unchanging cadence of the waves. Sitting upright, she leaned against the chain and rocked slightly. Her eyes closed gradually as the lazy summer rhythms worked their magic.

Sally opened her eyes sometime later to the realization that she wasn't alone anymore. A figure, barely discernible in the moonlight, crossed the front yard and walked down the side deck, carrying something. By his size and long-legged gait, she knew it was Tom.

She opened her mouth to call to him, but thought better of it when he stepped out onto the back deck, awash with moonlight, and she saw that he was naked.

6

SALLY WATCHED IN dazed silence as Tom tossed the bundle he'd been carrying—his clothes, it looked like—onto the picnic table he'd shoved against the wall earlier and ran his hands through his wet hair. He glistened with water, having obviously just emerged from the bay.

His resemblance to Michelangelo's *David* was now astoundingly complete. He had the most beautifully proportioned body she'd ever seen—powerful, graceful and layered with the kind of muscle you earned from physical labor.

Turning, Tom strode away from her, toward the outdoor shower. He turned on the water, hissing a curse when the cold spray hit him. Grabbing the soap, he lathered his hair and body with masculine efficiency, rinsed off and killed the water. He skimmed his hair back with both hands; the dark curls sprang stubbornly back up.

Sally felt a pinch of guilt for watching him unawares, but at the same time she couldn't wrest her gaze from him. It wasn't prurient interest—far from it. There was something about seeing him like this that made him seem both more vulnerable and more potently virile—and that made her feel strangely incomplete. There was an emptiness within her, a need so intense that it stole the breath from her lungs.

Dripping, Tom reached for the towel hanging on the shower head and briskly dried himself off from head to toe. Straightening, he slung the towel over his shoulders, turned in her direction...and stilled.

Sally found herself incapable of speech—or of rational thought, for that matter. She and Tom looked at each other across the darkened yard for a long moment, and then he slid the towel from his shoulders and wrapped it around his hips. He walked toward her slowly.

Standing over her, he wrapped one hand around the rusty chain and stroked her hair with the other. He smelled great; since when had plain old soap smelled so wonderful? "What are you doing out here?" he asked softly.

She found her voice. "Waiting for you."

He sighed. "We've done enough talking, don't you think?"

She met his gaze directly. "Yes."

Tom's eyes searched hers, as if to confirm that she meant what he thought she meant. Sally lifted his hand from her hair and pressed her lips to his palm.

Tom sank to his knees without breaking eye contact. He opened his mouth to speak, but he seemed to have trouble making up his mind what he wanted to say. Sally resolved the dilemma by leaning forward and brushing his lips with hers.

He returned the kiss, carefully framing her face in his hands, as if she were breakable—or as if the moment could disappear in a puff of smoke. His hands were still slightly damp, and cool to the touch, his lips searingly hot. Sally curled her hands lightly around his neck and felt his pulse quicken.

They kissed like this, softly and in charged silence,

until Sally grew dizzy with longing. Tom lowered a hand to her ankle, stroking upward to her knee, raising the hem of her long nightgown as he went. He pressed outward on her thigh very lightly, the pressure so subtle she could have ignored it if she wanted. She didn't.

She parted her legs and Tom moved between them, deepening the kiss. The coarse softness of the towel around his hips tickled her inner thighs, exposed by the hiked-up gown. He slipped his big hands beneath the gown, smoothing them over her hips, along the curve of her waist and up her back. It was a languid exploration, hypnotically slow, his curious hands stroking, massaging, speeding her heart and robbing her of breath.

"Are my hands too rough?" he whispered into her mouth.

"I like the way they feel."

"You feel incredible. So soft." He moved his hands around to the front, trailing his fingertips lightly over her belly. She closed her eyes and rested her hands on his shoulders, feeling the muscles flex with every slight movement of his arms. It felt breathtakingly intimate to be caressed this way underneath her nightgown, out here in the open, sitting on a swing with him kneeling between her legs. His hands no longer felt cool; they traced paths of heat wherever they touched.

Sally opened her eyes and met his gaze when he glided his fingertips along the undersides of her breasts. He grazed her nipples, sparking a pleasure so sharp that she hitched in her breath. He watched her, his eyes glittering darkly in the moonlight, his own breath coming fast, as he gently kneaded her breasts.

She drew him closer and kissed him again as he fondled her. Between her legs she felt the roughness of the terry cloth and the rigid flesh beneath it. Fumbling at his hips, she located the place where he'd tucked in the towel, and pulled; it came loose and dropped into the sand.

Tom kissed her throat and wrapped his hands around her hips, pulling her toward him slightly— just enough to feel the satin-smooth length of his erection against her damp heat. He rubbed against her, a slow, rhythmic slide of flesh against flesh that made her ache with feverish need.

Sally's breath came out in a soft moan. Tom looked into her eyes and shifted, nudging her with the broad head of his penis. He gripped her hips to hold her still on the unsteady swing. His shoulders tightened beneath her hands. He pressed into her, filling her slowly as she stretched around him.

He held her gaze until he was firmly seated within her, and then he lowered his head to hers again, wrapping his arms around her beneath her nightgown. Sally returned the embrace and they kissed and kissed, intimately connected but not moving. She felt ultrasensitized, acutely aware of the heat of his mouth, the cool caress of sand beneath her feet, the extraordinary pressure of his body penetrating hers.

He slid his hands down to her hips and rocked her slowly, the rusty chain squeaking as he glided in and out, in and out. Sally grabbed the chain with both hands and held on tight, trembling. As her arousal escalated, so did his. His breathing grew harsh, his thrusts more urgent. The armature of the swing set shook as he pounded into her; rusty metal creaked in an ever more frantic rhythm.

On the verge of release, Sally felt the right-hand chain go suddenly slack in her hand. A split second later, she was on her back in the sand, with Tom on top of her, the rusty metal having snapped under the strain they'd subjected it to.

"Are you all right?" Tom asked, still buried inside her; the fall hadn't separated them.

"Yes." She arched against him, pressing her hands to the small of his back, a silent entreaty.

He reached between them to stroke her lightly where they were joined. She writhed unselfconsciously beneath him as her pleasure mounted.

"You're so beautiful like this," he murmured. "I knew you would be." Without pausing in his intimate caress, he withdrew from her.

"No," she moaned, reaching for him.

"If I'm inside you when you come," he said softly, "I'll lose control—I won't be able to help it. And I'm not using anything." He lowered his mouth to hers, his deft fingers coaxing her closer, closer…

Her climax overtook her with such force that she cried out, clinging to him. As the pleasure subsided he whispered soothingly to her, holding her close, stroking her hair and back.

"You're wonderful," he murmured, nuzzling her neck. "So sexy. I want to make love to you all night."

"But if you don't have any, uh…"

"Condoms? I do." He nodded toward the picnic table on which he'd dumped his clothes. "Right over there in the pocket of my cutoffs."

She arched an eyebrow. "You've been carrying them around with you?"

Tom grinned. "A boy can always wish." He kissed her forehead, then stood and crossed to the deck. "And sometimes wishes even come true."

Sally considered the dire consequences of making love in the sand, an activity that Amber had once warned her about, then got up and followed Tom to the deck. He stood with his back to her, ripping open a packet he'd retrieved from his wallet. She gathered up her nightgown, pulled it off over her head and tossed it on the table along with his clothes.

Tom turned toward her and smiled. "Oh, yes. That's much better." He took her in his arms and kissed her, then lifted her onto the edge of the table, on top of their clothes. Stepping between her legs, he wrapped them around his waist and entered her in one deep, fluid stroke.

Tom kissed her hard, holding her tight. Easing her onto her back, he leaned over and took a stiff nipple in his mouth, teasing it with his lips and tongue. She raked her hands through his damp hair, banding her legs around him as the pleasure reignited, spiraling swiftly toward a second climax.

Scooping his hands under her hips, he lifted her so that each thrust sank deep. She'd never felt more possessed, more desired.

He moaned and arched over her, driving himself into her with a ferocity that felt almost desperate. The muscles of his shoulders and torso bulged beneath a sheen of perspiration. "Come again," he rasped. "I want to feel it."

"Yes," she whispered, and within seconds the pleasure gathered up and overflowed, shuddering through her. He grew very still, his gaze unfocused, his fingers digging into her hips. He groaned harshly as his body throbbed inside her, and then again, and again.

He collapsed on her, slick with sweat, his hands shaking as he gathered her in his arms. "I knew it would be like this," he whispered. "I knew it."

7

THE SUN WAS LOW in the sky the next afternoon when Sally braked her bike in front of the house and carried it through the front door. She was wheeling it past the living room to the hallway where she kept it when she stopped in her tracks.

A jar full of wildflowers stood in the middle of the coffee table. The flowers were a mixed assortment of the fragile little blossoms that dotted the grassy field next to the house. The jar still had dots of dried glue on it from where a label had been. A length of rough brown twine had been tied around the rim of the jar and knotted into a bow.

There were more flowers on the sideboard, sprouting from one of the blue-rimmed mugs; this time the bow had been fashioned from a heavy white cord, like clothesline. Another bouquet graced the dining table, this one gathered into a plastic tumbler bearing the likeness of Pocahontas and bedecked with several thicknesses of copper wire, again tied into a bow.

The ceiling groaned; Tom was walking around upstairs. Sally wondered whether he'd seen her return, and what he thought about the fact that she'd been gone all day. She stowed her bike away and went directly to the bathroom off the hall, where she stripped down and showered off the sweat from her marathon bike ride.

Wrapping a towel around herself, she went into her bedroom and stood in the doorway, blinking. More wildflowers had been scattered over her unmade bed, the sheets still rumpled from their love-making after they'd come inside last night.

They'd fallen asleep around dawn, their naked bodies contentedly entwined. When Sally awoke, the room was flooded with bright morning sunshine and Tom was gone. She'd heard the scrape of a hand saw upstairs and knew he was back at work. Remembering the night before—the swing, the picnic table, this bed—she'd felt again the heady thrill of his hands on her, his body inside her. She'd felt a connection with him—a bond between them—that had gone beyond the physical. Making love to Tom had deepened the rapport she'd experienced with him since the beginning, turning it into something more intimate—too intimate.

She'd showered, pulled on bike shorts and a T-shirt and ridden away to spend the day touring every bicycle path on the Cape, or most of them, anyway, in an attempt to buy some time alone to sort through her tangled emotions.

Did Tom feel what she felt? *Men aren't like us,* Amber had said. *If you offer this guy a friendly little summer romp with no emotional involvement, he'll jump at the opportunity.* But then, what was the deal with the wildflowers? And why had she felt so gratified to see them?

It'll never happen to me, she'd once vowed. *You can only fall in love with the wrong guy if you let yourself. I just won't let myself.* The trick now would be maintaining perspective—remembering that she went into this as a fling, not a relationship. Hopefully, that's all Tom was really after. The wildflowers were a sort of…courtesy, a way to say thank-you. She shouldn't make herself anxious by reading anything into them.

She threw on a loose sundress, which was old and worn but comfortable, and a zippered sweatshirt, because the air was turning cool. Returning to the living room, she stopped and stared through the rear sliding glass doors.

Huh?

She opened the door and walked barefoot out onto the deck, then stepped down into the sand and crossed to the swing set. The chain that had broken while they were making love on the swing had been repaired; the seat that should have been lying in the sand was drifting back and forth in the breeze off the bay.

"I fixed it."

Sally turned toward Tom's voice, which came from the upstairs deck. He stood leaning on the railing and looking down at her; he was dressed in khakis and a crisp white shirt with the sleeves rolled up to midforearm. She'd never seen him in anything other than workmen's grunge. With his classically chiseled looks, he could have been posing for a layout in *GQ*.

"I didn't expect you to fix it," she said. "I figured you'd just tear the whole thing down and throw it away."

He smiled. "It has sentimental value."

Her cheeks heated up.

Tom chuckled. "You really look outstanding when

you blush." He rubbed his neck. "Did you have a good bike ride?"

Sally hugged herself and nodded. "Thank you for the flowers. They're...thank you."

"I'd like to take you out to dinner."

So that's why he was all dressed up. *Please don't let him be wooing me*, Sally thought. "I had a burger about an hour ago."

"Ah." He nodded soberly. "Listen, the sun's about to set. Why don't we go watch it, and then we can take a walk on the beach?"

"Okay."

"Great." Tom kicked off his deck shoes, rolled up his pants and sprinted down the stairs.

They walked down to the beach and watched the spectacular orange-and-purple sunset with the crowd that had gathered. Tom threw a Frisbee for a while with two boys and their dog, and then he took Sally's hand and led her out into the bay. The placid water, which rose no higher than midcalf for hundreds of yards, had turned golden from the setting sun. Seaweed caressed their ankles as they walked.

"Look how far out we are," Tom said, pausing to squint at the shore. The few remaining people on the beach were indistinct little figures in the gathering dusk.

"It's so quiet out here." Sally rubbed her arms. "It's a little chilly this evening, though. You can tell fall is coming."

Tom drew her into his embrace and chafed her back and arms through her sweatshirt. "Do you want to head back?"

"No." Sally looped her arms around his waist and rested her head on his shoulder, reveling in his size and solidity. His shirt smelled comfortingly of laundry detergent and starch, and she felt his warmth through it.

He pressed his lips to her breeze-blown hair and then pushed it aside to kiss her forehead. She looked up and he closed his mouth over hers, holding her close. They kissed until they were breathless.

Why did this have to happen? she thought. *Why did I have to fall in love with him?* The thought ambushed her with such force that she drew back abruptly from Tom, shaken. She couldn't be in love with him. She wouldn't *let* herself be in love with him. That would ruin everything.

"What's wrong?" he asked.

"I…" She shrugged and studied the water lapping softly at their ankles. The rolled-up legs of his trousers had gotten a little damp.

She wrapped her arms around herself. He drew her toward him and cupped her head against his chest. "You're not having second thoughts, are you?" he asked. "Regretting last night?"

"No," she said quickly, but then she added, "not exactly."

He tilted her chin up so he could look in her eyes. "Which means…"

"Which means it would be better for me—for both of us—if we just…kept things light between us."

"A light relationship? Is that, like, half the calories and fat of a real relationship?"

"I'm serious."

"Yeah, I know, and I'm trying to work with you here, but somehow I don't think I'm gonna like your idea of light romance. Does the word *platonic* appear anywhere in the definition?"

"No."

"No?" He grinned and rubbed up against her suggestively. "It may not be that bad, then."

"What I mean is, I want to keep our relationship…friendly. Low-key. No commitment, no…" She groped for a way to say it without coming off like a cast-iron bitch.

"No *L* word?" Tom said.

"Right."

He regarded her soberly. "We may have a little problem, then."

"Why?"

"'Cause I'm already in love with you."

She closed her eyes. "Oh, no."

"Not quite the reaction I would have hoped for. Just do me one favor, Sally. Don't say 'Let's just be friends.' I really hate that."

"Tom, please. It would just be easier for me to handle…being with you…if we don't let ourselves get emotionally involved."

"You can set all the terms and conditions you want, but I'm already emotionally involved."

"I know. I…" *I am, too.* That's what she'd been about to say, but that would just complicate things. The point was to establish emotional distance between them; for that to work, her feelings would have to be kept under lock and key. "I just need this one favor from you, Tom. I need you to back off a little. Emotionally, not…"

"Not physically."

She was blushing again, damn it. "Right. We can still…"

"We can still screw," he said bluntly, "we just can't care about each other while we do it."

"Tom…"

"I've got news for you, sweetheart. That's not a 'favor,' it's a monumental sacrifice. You're asking me to pretend you mean nothing to me, that you're just another Mary Katherine Flaherty lifting her dress in the janitor's closet."

The image made Sally flinch, as he no doubt knew it would.

Tom took her by the shoulders and drilled his gaze into hers. Night was falling fast, but his eyes were incandescent in the purplish light of the setting sun. "That's bullshit, Sally, and you and I both know it." He never swore; he never used this tone with her. She'd really struck a nerve.

"It's the only way I can handle…" She gestured futilely with her hands.

"Sleeping with me? Yeah, but, see, sleeping together isn't…" He shook his head in evident frustration at the inadequacy of words. "It's not the *point* of us. The point of us is that we're in love."

"I never said—"

"Don't deny it. I'm not an idiot and neither are you. The point of us, the reason we click, is that we're in love, Sally. I love you. You love me. I didn't realize it until last night—until I was inside you, a part of you, and I realized how right it felt, how we fit together perfectly, how we belonged together. You didn't need to say anything—I knew you felt the same way."

Sally wanted to deny it, but the words wouldn't come.

"Now you're asking me to pretend I'm not in love with you. I can still sleep with you, but I've got to put on this big act like it doesn't mean anything."

"Maybe it means less than you think," she said. "Maybe your feelings—*our* feelings—are really more about hormones than love. Have you considered that?"

He propped his hands on his hips and regarded her with amused incredulity. "I think I know the difference between lust and love, Sally. I've been in lust pretty much continuously since around the age of fourteen. I've only been in love since I met you. I've never known a woman I was so compatible with."

"Sexually maybe."

"*Maybe?* What's a boy got to do to impress you?"

Sally smiled despite herself. "All right, definitely. Absolutely, no doubt about it, sexually we're—"

"Volcanic."

She cocked an eyebrow. "Volcanic?"

"'Explosive' didn't seem...messy enough." He gave her a bad-boy grin.

She rolled her eyes. "We're pretty messy together—I'll give us that."

"Last night I had the feeling you kind of liked it."

"I did. I do."

"Then what's this all about?" he asked, gentling his voice as he trailed a finger lightly down her face. "Why the cold feet?"

She sighed. "Can we walk a little farther out?"

"Sure." He curled an arm around her and they continued wading away from shore. They headed toward a dark form in the water that turned out to be a fairly large overturned rowboat. They found that it had become a home for a colony of shiny little black snails.

When they straightened up, Sally pointed to a glimmer of light about halfway up the Cape, barely visible on a dark strip of land that separated the night sky from the bay. "See that light there? The bright one? I grew up near there."

"On the beach, right?"

"Yep. Dad wouldn't have it any other way. Our bungalow...he loved it, but it was basically a hovel. All my male relatives are the same. If they have any ambition at all, it's for some idiotic goal, like becoming an international spy, or getting rich overnight. I can't remember a single one who ever held down a real job."

"Phil does."

"He's the exception. The women in my family seem destined to marry men with absolutely no future. Even my cousin Amber, who *swore* she'd hold out for a professional, ended up with this pathetically unfunny comic. Now she's stuck waiting tables in this little Debbie Does Dallas getup while Jimmy bombs in one club after another."

"Is she unhappy? Does she resent him?"

"Surprisingly, no. I mean, I would. But she's turned into this...this *doormat*, just like my mom and my aunts. It doesn't seem to bother any of them that they're bound in marriage to these dead-end guys—but I can tell you it bothers me. Always has. By the time I hit adolescence, all I wanted was a stable job with a regular paycheck—for me and...for anyone who was going to be a part of my life."

He nodded. "Then along comes messy old Tom O'Hearn swinging his toolbox and tearing everything apart."

"Something like that."

He tilted her chin up; his face looked almost ghostly in the moonlight. "I didn't plan on falling in love with you, Sally, and I'm sorry if it doesn't fit in with your plans. But I'll be damned if I'm going to give you up without a fight because of the career choices your father and uncles made."

"Those choices made me the person I am," she explained. "I care for you, but I can't get seriously involved with you. I can't deal with your kind of lifestyle—the uncertainty, the job insecurity...."

"The messiness?" Was he smiling? She couldn't tell.

"Not for the long haul."

"Just till the end of August?"

"Yes," she said quietly. "After that, it's over. It has to be. I could never accommodate myself to you. We'd only make each other miserable."

"I refuse to believe that. And I refuse to pretend you mean nothing to me when I'm head over heels in love with you."

She turned her back to him, hugging herself. "It's that or nothing, Tom. It's the only way I can feel okay about...being with you." She nudged the boat with her foot; it wouldn't budge.

He swore under his breath. "So that's it. If I stop telling you I love you, I can at least have part of you, if only for the next two weeks. I can have your body, but not your heart. But if I'm gonna keep inflicting my messy feelings on you, I don't even get that much."

She tried for a careless tone. "Most men wouldn't mind a couple of weeks of volcanic sex with no commitment."

"I'm not most men." He approached her from behind and stroked her hair. "And you're definitely not most women, or I wouldn't have fallen in love with you."

"Tom..."

"That's the last time I'll say it. You win, Sally. I can't just walk away from you—especially after last night." He reached around her to trail his hand down over a breast, molding it through her dress and sweatshirt. "I'm not saying it's enough. I want more from you than just sex. But if that's all you're offering, I guess I'll have to settle."

He kissed the back of her neck; she felt both relief and despair.

"Take off your panties," he said.

"What?"

"If sex is all we've got, I mean to make the most of our time together. Take off your panties."

Sally looked around. They were a quarter mile out in the moonlit bay. Even if the beach wasn't deserted, no one could see them. She lifted her dress, slid her panties down and stepped out of them. Tom took them from her and stuffed them in the pocket of her sweatshirt. Still standing behind her, he caressed her restlessly, squeezing her breasts, reaching under her skirt to slide a finger deep inside her. She threw her head back against his shoulder and moaned. He nipped her throat with his teeth.

"You're wet." He rocked against her as he coaxed her into a state of delirious need. She felt his hand between them, heard the rasp of his zipper. "Bend over," he said gruffly. "Hold on to the boat."

Sally did as he told her, parting her legs. Over his harsh breathing and the soft slap of water against the boat she heard the rip of plastic as he opened a condom. A moment later he threw her skirt up. The cool

night air on her naked flesh made her feel dangerously exposed, but before she could object, he seized
her hips and drove into her, groaning. She cried out
at the sense of invasion, so abrupt and yet so welcome, and again with each stabbing thrust.

"Is this enough?" he demanded breathlessly. "Is
this all you want from me?"

He wasn't so much making love to her as ravish-
ing her—taking what she offered with such mindless
fervor precisely because it was all she offered, all he
would ever have of her.

He reached around to caress her at the juncture of
her thighs. The first light stroke touched off such a
convulsive climax that her legs gave out and she slid
to her hands and knees in the water. Gripping her
around the waist, Tom knelt and hammered into her,
a low growl rising in his throat to become a shout of
fulfillment as his own release overtook him.

He withdrew from her almost immediately. She
heard him zip up his fly as she slumped down, trembling, into the water. Still breathing harshly, he
gained his feet and started wading back toward the
shore; she heard the steady splashing of his footsteps
receding behind her.

Sally felt cold and alone and wet. She began to
shake in earnest, and wrapped her arms around herself, squeezing her eyes shut, trying not to cry. She
knew she had to get up and walk back to the house,
but she'd be damned if she'd do it sobbing.

After about a minute, she heard the splashing
again, slower this time, growing louder as he approached.

"Sally?" Tom gathered her up in his big arms and
held her curled in his embrace as they sat waist-deep

in the shallow bay. He was shaking, too. "I'm sorry, sweetheart. I'm an idiot. Are you okay?"

She nodded.

"I shouldn't have done that," he said.

"It's all right."

"No it's not." He kissed her hair. "I shook you up. I shook *me* up. It's just that...I wanted more. I want more. It's not enough for me."

"I know."

"That's no excuse, though. If all we have is sex, then it should be better than that. It should be loving, not...whatever that was."

"Actually," she said, a little shyly, "it was kind of exciting."

"Yeah?" A chuckle rumbled in his chest. "I'll have to remember that. I aim to please, after all."

"You liked it, too. Admit it."

"You got me there." His arms tightened around her; she felt consumed by warmth despite the fact that she was sitting in the middle of the bay on a cool night. "But I would have liked it better if I'd been able to tell you how much I love—"

She pressed her fingers to his lips. "Tom..."

"I didn't say it," he retorted. "I just said I *wanted* to say it. So, by the strict letter of the law—"

"Can we stick to the spirit of the law here?" she implored. "Let's keep it low-key. Please."

"All right," he said. "For now."

She groaned. "Tom..."

"Hey, it won't be my fault if you just happen to come to the conclusion over the next couple of weeks that you can't live without me."

"How do you propose to pull that one off?"

"I may just have to make you my love slave." He

unzipped her sweatshirt and popped open the buttons of her dress.

"'Scuse me?"

"You know. Capture you in my erotic thrall and hold you there," he said matter-of-factly as he cupped her bare breast, teasing the nipple with his clever fingers. "Pleasuring you day and night with such passion and inventiveness that you can't bear to let me go, because no other man could ever hope to transport you to such heights of ecstasy."

"Okay…"

"You don't think I can do it." He scooped his free hand beneath her skirt, billowing on the surface of the water, and touched her lightly between her legs; she gasped, still slick and sensitized from their lovemaking.

"I don't know," she said with a sigh. "It might be worth a try."

"That's what I thought," he murmured, amusement in his voice as he caressed her slowly, rekindling the heat that he'd extinguished only minutes before. "Besides, it's a challenge. I could never resist a challenge."

8

"WOULD YOU MIND helping me with my suntan lotion?" Sally called from her bedroom.

"Is that a trick question?" Tom pushed away from the table where they'd shared a lunch of tuna sandwiches after a morning spent hanging cabinets in his kitchen upstairs. He'd kill the rest of the afternoon doing the detail work—sanding, staining and attaching hardware—but Sally had been itching to finish her novel down on the beach, and he'd encouraged her to indulge herself. Her Cape Cod vacation had turned into a working holiday, which she hadn't counted on, but had accepted with remarkably good grace. She deserved an actual afternoon in the sun, especially considering that her vacation would be over in a mere four days.

Four more days. Two weeks had passed since her ultimatum and his resolve to seduce her heart by seducing her body. In the beginning, the point had been to defeat her misgivings using the only weapon he was permitted—sex. The more they made love, he reasoned, the closer she would grow to him—intimacy of the body encouraging intimacy of the heart and mind.

That had been his theory. Practice had been something else again. He'd been indefatigable, and a good deal more imaginative than he'd ever been with any-one else—and she'd responded with equal enthusi-asm. They'd done things he'd never done before, us-ing positions he'd once considered physiologically impossible.

Which was all well and good—outstanding, as a matter of fact. Only, the sexual web he'd hoped to spin around Sally had captured him, as well. He was ensnared in a mesmerizing haze of sensuality the likes of which he'd never known, and it only in-creased his obsession with her.

Their prodigious lovemaking had deepened his commitment—hell, he was more than ready to pick out china patterns—but had it deepened hers? He hesitated to open a dialogue about it yet—given her past skittishness, she might freak out if she knew how serious he really was—but he felt sure she must be coming around. How could she not? There was more going on between them than sexual chemistry; there was a deep and profound bond. If he felt it, she must, too.

He found her sitting on the edge of her bed in that awesome purple bikini, rubbing sunscreen onto a supple brown thigh. With a carnal sigh, he knelt in front of her and took the bottle out of her hand.

"It's only my back I need help with," she said as he lifted her leg and propped it on his shoulder.

"I'll be the judge of that." He squeezed some of the coconut-scented lotion into his palm, rubbed his hands together and glided them up her runway-model legs. "I'm much more thorough than you are," he said, sliding his fingers beneath the leg hole of her bikini bottom.

"I've got a funny feeling I'm not going to be hitting the beach today," she said with a wry smile.

"You'll get out there," he said, smoothing lotion onto her other leg. "Eventually."

Finished with her legs, he squirted some lotion onto her upper chest and rubbed it in with lazy sweeps of his palms. When he reached the upper edge of her bikini top, he said, "This is in the way," and flicked open the gold, shell-shaped catch that secured it between her breasts. It sprang open, revealing her perky little breasts, milky white in contrast to her golden tan.

She rolled her eyes and reached for the bottle. "Give me that."

"No you don't." Tom caught her wrists in one hand and rose, pressing her back on the bed and straddling her hips. From across the house, the phone rang. "Don't even think about getting up to answer that." He lifted her arms over her head and held them down, which caused her back to arch provocatively. "You've entrusted me with a job, and I damn well intend to do it right."

She gasped when he dribbled a little lotion over her upthrust breasts. "That's cold."

"I can tell." He rubbed an erect nipple between his thumb and fingers until her breath caught. Leaning over, he sucked the other nipple into his mouth as he caressed her with a slippery hand. Her breath came in soft pants, and she writhed beneath him, but he kept her hands firmly pinned to the bed. Unable to hold out any longer, he thrust against her; her hips rose to meet him.

The answering machine kicked in on the fourth ring. From the living room came the tinny, breathless voice of a young woman. "Sally, omigod, he got it! He got the part! Call me!" *Click.*

"He got the part!" Sally exclaimed. She wrested her hands out of Tom's grip and sat up, looking ridiculously excited and pretty in nothing but her bikini bottom. "Jimmy got the part."

"Jimmy?"

"My cousin Amber's husband, the comic. He got a part in a TV show! That's so *great!*"

"Wait a minute. Isn't this the 'pathetically unfunny comic' you were telling me about?"

"Well…"

"And your cousin Amber, she's the doormat, right? The poor, misguided creature who thinks she's happy, but really can't be, 'cause she's married to a—what was it—dead-end guy with no future?"

Sally rolled her eyes. "All right, so maybe in this particular case, I jumped to conclusions—"

Three sharp raps sounded at the front door, and then came a slow creak as it opened. Tom's first thought was that he had to oil those hinges; his second thought was that someone was in the house.

"Hello? Sally?"

"Phil!" Sally whispered. Tom released her, and she leaped off the bed, yanking her bikini top closed as her cousin called her name, his footsteps growing louder.

"Take your time," Tom said. "I'll keep him out of

here." He left the bedroom and closed the door behind him.

"O'Hearn." Phil Owen stood in the hall, a walking cliché in tennis shoes, white knife-pleated shorts and a white polo shirt bearing an insignia that involved two crossed tennis rackets. His hair was sprayed-down smooth, his tan too flawless. He looked like that sexless doll that was supposed to be Barbie's boyfriend—Ken, that was his name.

"How's it goin', Phil?"

The men shook hands.

"So, uh…" Phil rubbed his hands thoughtfully and looked around. "Where's Sally?"

"She'll be out in a minute."

"She in there?" Phil strode toward the closed bedroom door, reaching for the handle.

Tom stepped in front of the door. "She'll be out in a minute. Want something to drink?"

Phil's gaze darted from Tom to the door and back to Tom. He turned and walked back down the hall. "I could use a cold vodka."

Tom followed him. "Sorry, no vodka. We've got cold beer, cold juice, cold soda—"

Phil glanced over his shoulder, his expression blank—too blank.

We. Tom hadn't meant to advertise his relationship with Sally, but there it was. What did it matter if Phil knew, anyway?

"What kind of beer?" Phil asked.

"Dos Equis."

"What is that—that Mexican stuff?"

"It's great."

Phil grimaced. "I'll have some of that, if it's all you've got." He looked around the renovated kitchen and peered through the glass door at the new deck. Tom retrieved the beer from the fridge; he and Sally had consolidated their provisions down here given that his kitchen was in a state of flux. "Place doesn't look the same."

High praise. "That was the point, wasn't it?" Tom handed him the beer.

Phil looked at the bottle as if it were something the neighbor's dog had left in the backyard. "I'd like a glass, if you don't mind."

Sure thing, Phil, old boy. "Comin' right up."

"Hi, Sally." Phil spared a tight-lipped smile for Sally as she entered the kitchen, looking cool and pristine in white shorts and a white-and-pink-striped T-shirt.

"Hi, Phil." Sally didn't so much as glance in Tom's direction as she crossed to her cousin and pecked him on the cheek. "Did you enjoy the safari?"

"Do you have any idea how big insects grow in Africa?"

"Uh…"

"I've only got about twenty minutes here," Phil said, consulting his Rolex. "I'm meeting a client at his club for lunch and a set of tennis. We're playing double or nothing for his fee."

"Yeah, I noticed your tennis whites." Sally did glance at Tom then, her gaze sweeping quickly, almost imperceptibly, over his ripped gray T-shirt, paint-spattered cutoffs and prehistoric work boots.

He wondered what she was thinking. Or maybe he didn't want to know.

Phil accepted the glass of beer from Tom and sipped it daintily. "I just thought I'd stop by and see how the house turned out. Who bought the furniture?"

"Me." Sally's brow furrowed. "You."

Tom wished Phil didn't have the power to make her nervous. "She's got a real eye for decorating," Tom said. "I think it looks great."

Phil nodded thoughtfully as he strolled through the living room, now a thousand times brighter than it had been a month ago, with white walls, colorful rugs and well-stuffed sofa and chairs. "Not what I would have picked, but not too bad."

"Uh, thanks," Sally muttered.

"How come the swing set's still out there?" Phil asked, squinting through the glass door. "Damn thing's an eyesore."

Smiling, Tom tried to catch Sally's eye. "Gee, I kind of like—"

"He's going to take it out," Sally said quickly. "He just hasn't gotten around to it yet."

"See that you do," Phil said, heading for the stairway. "I take it the upper level is furnished the same way."

"Um...similar," Sally said, sprinting up the stairs after her cousin. "Or it will be, when we get the furniture unpacked and set up."

Tom sighed and followed them to the second floor.

"Looks like shit," Phil pronounced, weaving

around piles of discarded kitchen fixtures and old floor tiles.

Sally turned crimson. "It's not finished yet."

"Obviously." Phil peered at Tom over the top of his glass as he took another sip of beer. "When were you planning on wrapping this up, O'Hearn?"

Tom met Phil's gaze steadily. "By August thirty-first. You haven't changed the deadline on me, have you?"

"Nobody can get that much done in—what? Four days?"

Tom crossed his arms without averting his gaze. "I can."

"I'm sure you're a very hard worker," Phil said in tones just this side of smarmy condescension. "That's why I hired you. But four days—I don't think you realize how short a period of time that really is."

Tom clenched his jaw. "I own a calendar, Phil."

Phil turned to Sally. "You've been supervising his work. Can he do it?"

"Yes. Absolutely. He works from dawn till dusk."

"And he'll clean up after himself? He'll haul away all the debris?"

"Of course," she assured him. "I'm sure he'll leave the place absolutely—"

"Excuse me," Tom interjected, "but would you two mind not talking about me as if I wasn't standing right here?" *You two.* Tom's gaze took in the two cousins, who looked eerily alike right now, with their similar coloring and attire. They put him in mind of a married couple heading out for an afternoon at the club. In fact, Phil Owen was exactly the kind of man

Sally had always planned on ending up with—a stable professional with a steady income and clean fingernails.

To her credit, Sally's blush deepened. "I'm sorry, Tom. I didn't mean—"

"You don't have to apologize to this guy," Phil told her. "He was hired to do a job by a certain date. He's got to expect to have his work evaluated. He knows better than anyone how much is riding on this job."

The Livermore Building was riding on this job, Tom though, and his career was riding on the Livermore Building. It was his chance to prove himself, to establish his reputation in historic renovation. He had to snag that contract. Phil knew that, the arrogant bastard, and he was using that knowledge to turn the screws on Tom—for no other reason than that he got off on lording it over his inferiors.

With a thin smile in Tom's direction, Phil started down the stairs. "Why don't you explain to me what you've done to the downstairs deck? Looks like you've taken a few liberties."

Sally started after him. "I told Tom he could—"

"I'll speak for myself, Sally." Tom grabbed her hand and pulled her back. "We'll be down in a minute, Phil."

Phil paused halfway down the stairs to look back up at them, arching one eyebrow the way Sally always did when something struck her as curious. Tom realized what had captured Phil's attention when Sally yanked her hand out of his grasp and backed away from him.

"What do you know, Sally?" Phil's gaze slid back and forth between Sally and Tom. His mouth twitched, but his eyes remained hard. "I was worried you'd be bored here, but it looks as if you've kept yourself busy. I'll be waiting downstairs."

Sally stalked down the hall, hugging herself. Tom followed her into his bedroom. She closed the door behind them. "He knows."

"Yeah, so?"

She stared at him. "Did you tell him?"

"About us? Not in so many words, but I guess I let it slip."

"Great." She turned her back and paced away. "That's just great. He thinks I'm a complete slut now."

Heat prickled Tom's ears. "Because you're sleeping with the help?"

"That's how he views it."

"Is that how you view it?"

She let out an unsteady breath and turned to face him. "You know how I view it."

"No, I don't." He took a step toward her; she took a step back. "Frankly, I've been more than a little curious lately about your views."

"I don't understand."

He closed his hands over her shoulders. "What's happening between us, Sally?"

She twisted out of his grip and backed up. "You know what's happening between us. We discussed it. We came to an understanding."

"That was two weeks ago. Things have changed since then."

"Nothing's changed, Tom." She turned and looked out the window, her voice strained, her arms tightly banded around her.

"You can't mean that."

"We agreed we weren't going to get seriously involved."

"I was already seriously involved," he said. "I never made any secret of that. And you were, too. You still are. You just won't admit it."

"We agreed it was just going to be sex."

"No, you said it was just going to be sex." He came up behind her. She spun around and tried to sidestep him, but he slammed both hands on the window frame, trapping her. "I went along because it was that or nothing, and I couldn't bear the idea of giving you up completely. And I thought...I hoped...you'd come around eventually."

"And I hoped you'd be able to keep it in perspective, to keep to our agreement."

Tom lowered his head and closed his eyes, struggling to understand her fears, to give her every benefit of the doubt, even though a little despairing voice was telling him this was it—it was over. "I know it's thrown you for a loop, having Phil show up like this. And I know you never expected to fall for a guy like me, and you're kind of freaking out here, but—"

The door swung open; Phil stood there, smirking at them. "Can you hurry it up? I've got to be out of here in ten minutes."

"Get lost, Phil," Tom said over his shoulder.

"We'll be right down." Sally ducked under Tom's

arm and started toward the door as Phil turned and left.

Tom grabbed Sally's arm and swung her around. "I thought you would have figured out by now that I'm not your father or one of your hapless uncles."

"Nine minutes!" Phil called out from the stairs.

"Let me go, Tom," Sally said quietly.

Tom held her gaze for an interminable moment and then dropped his hand from her arm. She went downstairs. He sat on the edge of his bed and rubbed his neck for a minute, and then he went to the closet and got his duffel bag down from the shelf. It took about another minute to dump the contents of his dresser drawers into the bag and zip it up.

"Where do you think you're going?" Phil asked when Tom came downstairs with the bag. Sally just stared at him.

"Boston."

Phil and Sally followed him outside. He opened the door of his pickup truck and tossed the duffel bag onto the passenger seat.

"What about the house?" Phil demanded. "You're going to leave it like this?"

"I've got things to do in Boston," Tom lied. He climbed into the driver's seat, pulled the door closed and rolled down the window. "I'll be back to finish the house in a couple of weeks."

Sally closed her eyes. When she opened them, they were dark with emotion. She mouthed his name. He looked away and fished his keys out of his pocket.

"Leaving things undone and coming back in a

couple of weeks wasn't part of our agreement," Phil said.

"Yeah, well, I'm not very good about keeping to agreements." Tom twisted the key in the ignition; the engine rumbled to life. "Ask your cousin."

Sally covered her mouth with her hand and studied the crushed shells beneath her feet.

Phil said, "As far as I'm concerned, O'Hearn, you're walking out on the job. If you drive away now, you can kiss the Livermore contract goodbye."

Tom put the truck in reverse and raised his middle finger in a parting salute. "Kiss this," he said, and drove away.

9

SALLY SAT on the front stoop with her head in her hands, listening to Phil rant and rave about Tom.

"And that's another thing!" Phil exclaimed, pacing back and forth in the sandy front yard. "He's insolent. Always has been. There's that edge to him, like he can't accept that I'm the one calling the shots, I'm the one with the deep pockets. Used to be you hired a guy to make repairs and he called you 'sir' and acted like he meant it."

"Tom can't act," Sally muttered.

"What?"

She looked up at Phil, looming over her in his ridiculous tennis costume and checking his watch for the tenth or eleventh time. "He can't act," she repeated wearily. "He can't pretend. It's not in his nature."

I refuse to pretend you mean nothing to me, he'd said, *when I'm head over heels in love with you.* God, what had she been thinking, to let him drive away like that? What was the matter with her?

"Pretense is part of life," Phil said. "If you're hiring yourself out to fix stuff up, you've got to at least pretend to be deferential to your clients, even if it's not in your nature. That's part of the game. If Tom

O'Hearn can't handle that, maybe he went into the wrong line of business."

"How can you say that? You've seen his work. He's brilliant at what he does."

"He's competent."

She stood up. "He's incredible. Not only does he work his butt off, he's smart, creative—"

"Look, Sally." Phil cocked his head, his expression all too knowing. "It's none of my business if you want to boff the guy. I'm open-minded."

"Oh, *please.*"

"You find yourself sharing a house with a hunk in a leather tool belt..." He shrugged. "It would be like me finding out there's...I don't know, a topless dancer living upstairs. I'd go for it, too. I don't blame you for a second."

"You're a real piece of work, you know that, Phil?"

"All I'm saying is, I understand about recreational sex. A little friendly nookie and no strings. I'm a big fan of it myself—that's something you and I have in common."

"Oh, God." Sally sank down on the stoop again and replaced her face in her hands. "What have I done?"

Phil squatted in front of her and said, in a solicitous tone, "But you can't let your hormones start doing your thinking for you. That's when you get into trouble. Take this Tom O'Hearn. I'm sure he's dynamite in the sack, but the bottom line is he's a total loser."

She uncovered her face. "How can you say that? You hardly know him."

"I know his type." Phil laid a brotherly hand on her shoulder. "And so do you. All too well."

"No."

"A friendly piece of advice, Sally. Don't make the same mistake Amber did. Ditch this guy. You can do better."

"I blew it. I totally blew it." Tears burned Sally's eyes; she couldn't swallow.

"Sally?" Phil crouched down, tilted her head up and shoved his watch in her face. "I've got to go. Pull yourself together." He patted her on the shoulder, stood up and walked over to his car.

"Give him the Livermore contract, Phil."

"No." He slid behind the wheel. "Ciao."

She got up and swiped at her tears. "You're a shallow, heartless son of a bitch, Phil Owen, and if there's a hell, you'll probably end up there."

"Yeah, but in the meantime I get to wear a Rolex and drive a fifty thousand dollar car." He turned on the engine, which purred silkily. "Life's full of trade-offs."

She crossed the sandy yard to lean on the open window of Phil's car. "Give him the contract, Phil."

"Why?"

"Because he deserves it, and it's the fair thing to do."

"Life's not fair."

"Then do it because it would be a good deed. Wouldn't you like to see how it feels to do a pure, unselfish thing, just once?"

"Sure, but what's in it for me?"

"See, maybe we need to define our terms here.

'Unselfish' means there *isn't* anything in it for you. You're just doing it because it's the right thing." Although, in this case, the right thing was also the best thing for Phil, because Tom was the best man for the Livermore job, but Sally was loath to ruffle Phil's feathers by harping on that.

"I don't know," Phil grumbled, smoothing down his hair in the rearview mirror. "All this warm and fuzzy crap. No good can come of it."

"Do it for me," she said. "I know you feel some family loyalty. It's just about your only decent trait. Do it because it'll make me happy."

Phil rolled his eyes. "Oh, what the hell. All right, I'll hire him for the Livermore job."

"Oh, thank you, Phil!" Leaning through the car window, she clumsily embraced her cousin as tears spilled down her face.

"Hey hey *hey!*" Phil pushed her away roughly and rubbed at a tiny dark spot on the upholstery. "No tears on the leather!"

She wiped her face on her sleeve. "Would you give me his number in Boston so I can call him and tell him he's got the job?"

With a disgusted sigh, Phil popped the glove compartment open, pulled out a leather business-card case and flipped through it. "Here." He handed her a plain white card imprinted with TOM O'HEARN, and below that, S•P•O•O•S•E. At the bottom was an address on Acorn Street in Boston and a phone number.

"Adios!" Phil waved as he backed away. "See you at the next wedding."

IT WAS TEN O'CLOCK that night when Sally finally got through to Tom. She'd dialed his number repeatedly over the past few hours, but it just rang and rang; evidently he wasn't one for answering machines. Not expecting an answer, she had her mouth full of Ben and Jerry's Cherry Garcia ice cream when, after three rings, she heard Tom's voice: "Hello."

She struggled to swallow.

A hint of irritation: "Hello?"

"Tom?"

There came a moment of silence, just a little too long. "Sally?"

"Hi."

Another pause. "Hi."

Now that she had him on the line, Sally found the challenge of stringing words together almost insurmountable. "I must have dialed your number about a hundred times. How come it took you so long to get there?"

"I stopped and visited a friend in Plymouth."

"Ah." A woman. He'd stopped to see a woman, an old girlfriend probably. Sally remembered the way his hands had felt that afternoon, slick with suntan lotion. She felt as if she'd been kicked in the stomach.

"My old college roommate, Dan Draper," Tom said. "He'd asked me to stop by on my way back. His wife makes a mean pot roast, and I ended up hanging out and talking on their back porch for a few hours."

"Oh. Good. I mean, I'm glad you ate."

After another hesitation, Tom said, "Sally, why did you call?"

"I called to tell you that Phil's decided to give you the Livermore job."

"Yeah?"

"Yeah."

"Did you talk him into it?"

"Yeah, I guess."

He gave an extended sigh. "I appreciate the effort, Sally, but you can tell Phil to take that job and shove it."

"What? You were desperate for that job. You said it would establish your reputation. You said—"

"I said a lot of stuff before I realized what a snake that guy is, and how nuts it would be for me to work for him. One of us would end up dead from multiple stab wounds before that project was over."

"What about your career?"

"I'll just have to find another high-profile job to prove myself on. It's not like that's the only old building in Boston."

"Are you sure?"

"Yeah. Like I said, thanks for doing what you did, but it wouldn't work out." He yawned. "Look, I'm kind of beat, with all the driving and whatnot, so if you don't mind, I'm gonna say goodbye now—"

"I also wanted to talk about…us." She really should have rehearsed this part; she didn't have the slightest idea what to say or how to say it.

"Don't, Sally."

"But—"

"We've talked everything through. There's nothing more to say."

"No, but I think there is. I mean, there are things I want to say. Things I should have said before—"

"Sally, you don't have to rehash it. Maybe I was a little slow on the uptake for a while there, but I did finally get the point. You're right—it was dumb for us to get involved."

"Tom…"

"Want a chuckle? I came that close to asking you to marry me."

The breath left Sally's lungs.

"I'm gonna unplug the phone and get some sleep now." Softly he added, "Have a good life, Sally."

Click.

10

SALLY STOOD IN THE DARK on the front steps of the handsome, ivy-festooned brick town house on Acorn Street, ringing the doorbell. No answer. She held her watch in the corona of light from the brass door lamp: 2:00 a.m. She'd driven for hours to get here, and now he wasn't even home. In her mind's eye she saw Tom slathering Hawaiian Tropic on some faceless woman who was, of course, petite and voluptuous.

Sally rang the bell again. He wasn't home. She looked up and down the street, impressed that Tom O'Hearn lived here on this narrow, picturesque cobblestone lane in Boston's most distinguished historic district. She turned the doorknob. No luck; it was locked.

There was a window next to the front door, with old-fashioned venetian blinds on the inside. After another furtive glance at the street, she pushed it upward. It moved.

She shoved the window all the way open and climbed awkwardly through, grateful for her long legs, because the sill was a fair distance above the brick sidewalk. The blinds clattered as she tumbled through, landing painfully on the floor. *Success!*

Gaining her feet, she closed the window, tidied the blinds and looked around.

By the moonlight filtering in stripes through the half-closed blinds she saw a high ceiling with decorative moldings, a polished hardwood floor and a fireplace with a beautifully carved mantel...but no furniture. A ladder stood against one wall and there was a wadded-up tarp in a corner. She smelled a faint whiff of new paint; he'd probably painted before leaving for the Cape at the beginning of August.

Room after room looked much the same, although she did find a table and chairs in the kitchen, and a sofa, desk and numerous cartons of books in a back room with high, multipaned windows.

Ducking beneath some elaborate scaffolding, she climbed the stairs to the second floor. In the largest bedroom, which contained another spectacular fireplace, she discovered an unmade but very inviting-looking sleigh bed. The sheets were soft white cotton, the quilt handmade.

She sat on the edge of the bed and felt tired—bone weary, in fact—for the first time that night. After a moment's thought, she muttered, "What the heck," peeled off her clothes, got into the bed and pulled up the covers.

IT WAS CLOSE TO THREE in the morning when Tom wheeled his bike in through the back door and parked it in the kitchen. Unable to sleep, he'd spent a couple of hours riding through the city's parks, which usually tired him out just fine—but right now he felt even more wired than when he'd started out.

He couldn't stop thinking about Sally, wondering how long it would take to get her out of his system. He had no experience to go on, having never been in love before. How long did it take for the agonizing void inside to start healing? Months? Years? Right now he couldn't imagine ever being over her.

Dan Draper, infinitely more experienced with women, had assured him that a clean break would be less painful in the long run. That made sense to Tom, which was why he'd hustled Sally off the phone when she called earlier—although, as soon as he hung up, he'd regretted it. Would he ever hear her voice again?

Cursing under his breath, he made his way in the dark to the staircase, under the scaffolding and up to his bedroom.

Tom whipped off his denim jacket as he entered the room, and was about to toss it on the bed when he stopped in his tracks; the jacket dropped from his hand and landed in a heap on the floor. He stood there staring at her for a full minute while his mind flip-flopped back and forth between *Thank God she came* and *Why did she have to come?*

He approached the bed slowly, as if its occupant—barely visible in the hazy moonlight—were an apparition that would vaporize at any moment. She was asleep on her back, the covers drawn up above her breasts, her arms arching gracefully over her head. Her face was turned toward him, her hair a spray of gold on the pillow.

Tom sat on the edge of the bed. She opened her

eyes and whispered his name, her voice sleepy soft. "Where have you been?" she asked.

"Biking around the city." He ran a finger lightly along her cheek, warm and rosy from sleep. "What are you doing here, sweetheart?"

She sat up, her expression sheepish, her hair all over the place; she'd never looked more beautiful. "I had to see you." Holding the covers over her breasts—silly, really, considering their past—she curled her hand around his neck and pulled his head to hers. Before he could react, she kissed him, and he returned the kiss with enthusiasm.

It was sweet and warm and wonderful and he loved it, but he drew back first, shaking his head. "Sally—"

"Shh." She pressed her fingers to his lips, and then she lowered her hand to his shirt and slid the top button out of its buttonhole.

"No, Sally." He took her hand and lowered it to her lap, enclosing it in both of his. "This isn't a good idea."

A look of hurt flickered across her features.

"It's not that I don't want you," he said, stroking her hair. "You can't imagine how much I want you. I'll never stop wanting you, not as long as I live. But the thing is, I want more than just your body. I'm self-ish—I want all of you."

"Tom…"

"No, let me talk, Sally, because we have to get this clear between us. It's not gonna work, dragging things out like this. I can't abide by your terms and conditions anymore—no commitment, no declarations of love. I can't pretend I don't care."

"I know. Actually, that's part of the reason I came—to tell you I've thrown out my old conditions. I have new ones."

He regarded her suspiciously. "New ones?"

"One, actually. Something you have to agree to before I'll let you have your way with me."

A gust of laughter escaped him. "Have my *way* with you?"

She nodded. "Marriage."

He stared at her in shock. "Did you say…"

She bit her lip. "Am I moving too fast for you?"

"Actually, I think you may have just caught up with me." He smiled and began unbuttoning his shirt. "Welcome to hyperspace."

MEN at WORK

All work and no play?
Not these men!

July 1998

MACKENZIE'S LADY by Dallas Schulze

Undercover agent Mackenzie Donahue's
lazy smile and deep blue eyes were his best
weapons. But after rescuing—and kissing!—
damsel in distress Holly Reynolds, how could
he betray her by spying on her brother?

August 1998

MISS LIZ'S PASSION by Sherryl Woods

Todd Lewis could put up a building with ease,
but quailed at the sight of a classroom! Still,
Liz Gentry, his son's teacher, was no battle-ax,
and soon Todd started planning some
extracurricular activities of his own....

September 1998

A CLASSIC ENCOUNTER
by Emilie Richards

Doctor Chris Matthews was intelligent, sexy
and *very* good with his hands—which made
him all the more dangerous to single mom
Lizette St. Hilaire. So how long could she
resist Chris's special brand of TLC?

Available at your favorite retail outlet!

MEN AT WORK™

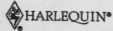 HARLEQUIN®  Silhouette®

Look us up on-line at: http://www.romance.net

PMAW2

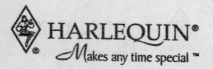

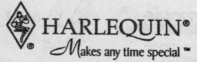

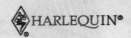
HARLEQUIN®

Not The Same Old Story!

 PRESENTS®
Exciting, glamorous romance stories that take readers around the world.

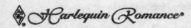
Sparkling, fresh and tender love stories that bring you pure romance.

Bold and adventurous—Temptation is strong women, bad boys, great sex!

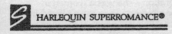
Provocative and realistic stories that celebrate life and love.

Contemporary fairy tales—where anything is possible and where dreams come true.

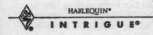
Heart-stopping, suspenseful adventures that combine the best of romance and mystery.

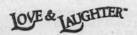
Humorous and romantic stories that capture the lighter side of love.

COMING NEXT MONTH

#697 A BODY TO DIE FOR Kate Hoffmann
Hero for Hire

When bodyguard Jackson Beaumont discovered he'd be guarding
Judge Lamar Parmentier, he never suspected the judge was a
corpse! Or that the late judge's widow would be so young, so
gorgeous, so irresistible…. But Madeline Parmentier had a secret.
And until Jackson figured out what she was hiding, he didn't dare
trust her with his heart—or his life!

#698 TAKEN! Lori Foster
Blaze

Virginia Johnson ran a huge corporation—she was a woman in
control. Until Dillon Jones—whose job description *wasn't* listed in
the Fortune 500—kidnapped her. Suddenly she was at the mercy of
a powerfully sexy man who kept her both captive…and captivated.

#699 SINGLE SHERIFF SEEKS… Jo Leigh
Mail Order Men

Single sheriff Dan Collins was seeking some peace and quiet. That
ended when the townsfolk placed his personal ad in *Texas Men*
magazine. Coincidentally, Dan stumbled upon his most bizarre
case ever—and one very single sexy suspect. What could Dan do
but stick *closer-than-this* to gorgeous Annie Jones?

#700 THE LAST BACHELOR Carolyn Andrews

Mac Delaney couldn't believe it—he'd lost all his poker buddies to
matrimony! But Mac wasn't about to let any woman drag him to
the altar *ever*. Then he met gorgeous Frankie Carmichael, and was
ready to kiss the single life goodbye…till he discovered Frankie
had *no* desire to walk down the aisle either!
